The Second-Chance Summer

A SWEET, SMALL-TOWN ROMANCE

WINTERVALE PROMISES
BOOK NINE

MELODIE MARCH

"Harley! Wake up, man. Do you seriously not hear that?"

Harley Thatcher woke up to his friend Rick shaking his shoulder a little roughly. He was just about to give Rick crap about it when he realized that the station house alarm was going off.

"Dang it," Harley grumbled as he jumped to his feet and followed Rick to get their gear. He didn't even remember falling asleep, now that he thought about it. *How did I sleep through that alarm?* Harley tried to shake himself awake as he climbed into his boots, then pants and suspenders, before slipping into his jacket.

"Thatcher! You're in the engine with me," his Captain called back to him as he was gathering up his gear. Harley finally focused for a minute so he could hear the call over the alarm. Based on the address, it sounded like there was a fire at a junkyard that was only a few blocks from a residential neighborhood. Harley started running to the engine as he finished putting on his jacket; there was no time to waste.

The drive to the junkyard, mostly full of broken down old cars but notorious for public health code violations involving flammable chemicals, was a tense one. Harley and his engine company were silently preparing for the worst case scenario. If there *were* toxic chemicals on the property, there was a possibility that a fire could not only burn out of control, but spread to the nearby houses.

"What's the plan, Cap?" asked Harley's best friend, Miguel, from the back of the engine. "This is our third call there this year."

"Let's assess this particular situation first and then we can worry about turning them over to public health again," the Captain answered, a hint of exasperation in his voice. When they pulled up to the junkyard, the gate wasn't even locked. They could already see a fire burning toward the back, near one of their many ancient compactors. The Captain called out for backup as they approached the fire. Even from a distance, they could smell gasoline in the air and that meant this fire was going to burn fast and hard. There was no way to predict the behavior of a fire in a situation that was practically made to feed its insatiable hunger.

Everyone jumped out with the knowledge that they couldn't use water to fight a fire like this. Water was only going to make things worse and that meant they would have to fight the fire with chemicals. But until the backup came, it was going to be a game of tag and Harley's company was starting from behind. Everywhere they looked, there was another car, primed to explode at any minute. Even as the heat cut through his suit and down to his skin, it was hard to deny the adrenaline high that came from facing down the all-consuming act of nature in front of him.

It was easy to be cocky... they were the good guys. They always beat the fire. Harley had been at his station in Austin for six years and while he'd had a few close calls, the company hadn't lost a single soul yet. He wasn't going to break their record tonight. The sound of sirens from other trucks were sounding in the distance as everyone from his station started prepping the rest of their gear.

"Think there is anyone in there?" Miguel yelled over the noise of the flames and crunching metal.

"Nah, the owner of this miserable place leaves at five and makes his employees follow. No overtime. It's how it got so overrun," the Captain answered through the headsets. "Let's get started. Everyone, triple check your PPE and your oxygen levels. I don't want any of this fire to make it over to that neighborhood, am I understood?"

"10-4, cap!" the whole station answered.

Harley was just about to follow his fellow firefighters into the junkyard when suddenly, from somewhere nearby, he heard a voice. It was muffled by his helmet but he could still hear it.

"Help! Please! I'm stuck!"

The Captain heard it too. "Thatcher," he said through his headset, "go see where it is. Miguel, go with him."

"No," Harley quickly countered. "You worry about the fire. If I need help, I'll grab someone off one of the other trucks. I've got this covered."

Without a second look, Harley turned on his heel and ran in the direction of the voice. He was getting closer, but the voice was getting fainter, and when he finally found its source, he knew why. A teenage boy was on the ground with his leg pinned under the entire front half of a rusted out old car. When they locked eyes, the boy's eyes registered relief but his pale face was heavy with exhaustion.

"My name is Harley Thatcher and I'm going to help you. How long have you been here, kid?" Harley asked as he lifted up his mask. The boy shook his head.

"I don't know. Wade, the owner, he pays me a few dollars to help gather scrap metal. I forgot my house keys in the office so I came back and there was an explosion. I don't even know how but suddenly there was a car on top of me. I just want to go home," the boy said, trying desperately to look tough and failing.

Harley was just about to tell the boy it was going to be okay. Once the other trucks pulled up, it would only take four or five firefighters to safely lift the car off his leg so the EMTs could get him to the hospital. But then, Harley felt the ground begin to rumble beneath them...

The last thing he was aware of before he lost consciousness was a blast of pure white hot heat against his cheek. And then, everything went black.

Chapter One

JUNIPER - SIX MONTHS LATER

Juniper Larson could feel her calf muscles beginning to tense up as she leaned against the outside wall of Wren & Candle, her farm-to-table restaurant. She pulled an old handkerchief out of the pocket of her shorts and wiped away the sweat that was pouring down her brow. Lunch service at the restaurant Juniper had opened in a refurbished barn on Wintervale Farms was always chaotic. The farm had been in Juniper's family for several generations but the restaurant was her idea. Every dish was made from produce grown just a few steps away from Wren & Candle, and everything else was brought in exclusively from other farms in Vermont. The restaurant, which sat right on the border of Wintervale and the resort town of Hadleigh, was an instant success. It was everything Juniper had dreamed of...

It was just really exhausting.

Wintervale Farms was more than Wren & Candle. Juniper's great-grandparents founded the farm over a hundred years ago and it passed down through the family ever since. It began as a horse farm with a carrot patch in the back and slowly grew over the years to what it was now; the stables and carrots were still there, but so was an apple orchard, an acre of varied seasonal vegetables, a pumpkin patch, a greenhouse, and now, the restaurant. The family's old farmhouse sat close to the stables, but far enough away from the usual foot traffic that even during their busiest times, it never felt like they lived in a tourist attraction. Juniper was grateful for that, because the home that her great-grandfather had built from the ground up had been her haven since she was a little girl.

The slowly-creeping heat of June was starting to prick at Juniper's skin and suddenly, she was as hot outside as she had been inside, so that meant it was time to get back to work. Because the back of the barn was taken up by a reasonably-sized kitchen, the seating space inside of Wren & Candle was small. While it meant reservations were considered a precious commodity, it also meant that when the space filled up in the summer, it got steamy and it happened fast. Even the ceiling fans and small AC units in the window weren't terribly useful come July and August. And this was shaping up to be a hot summer.

As soon as Juniper stepped into the restaurant, her manager/host, Sebastian, stopped her before she could even pass the host's station.

"Juniper, Claudia and Frannie got here while you were down getting tomatoes. They just want to say hi," he said as he replaced a stack of menus. "Also, you told me to remind you when it was one o'clock, and it's almost one o'clock."

Juniper looked at her watch and sighed. Claudia was one of her best friends from high school and while Frannie was a transplant from New York who just moved to Wintervale, they'd grown close quickly. She wanted to sit down with them and have a cold glass of Wren & Candle's signature homemade lemonade, but she needed to be back at the house at one. Juniper let out a sigh and hurried over to the one small separate table they kept empty for friends or VIPs who dropped in. When Claudia and Frannie saw her, they smiled, but Juniper saw the concern in Claudia's face.

"Girl," she said as Juniper slid in the chair next to her, "you look like you've been running a marathon with the flu. Are you sick?"

Juniper laughed. "It's just been a long morning but thank you for the confidence boost." Frannie reached across the table and tucked two sweaty strands of Juniper's hair behind her ears.

"You look as gorgeous as ever, but maybe you've just been running yourself a little ragged lately?" Frannie posed it as a question but Juniper knew it wasn't.

"You know how summer is around here. I get a few college kids who sign up for the summer job and then they realize that picking peppers and green beans in the sun isn't a goof around job. Suddenly, it's just me and my year round crew doing the work of fifteen people. Plus, my stablehand quit to move to Vietnam."

Claudia and Frannie shared the same look of shock. Juniper didn't even bother waiting for them to ask.

"Apparently, the surf is better there? And he decided he wants to be a surfer now, not a large animal vet. That means once Rose gets here, I have to go straight to the stables. Oh, crap. What time is it?"

Everyone looked at their watch or phone at the same time.

"One," Claudia answered, which sent Juniper sliding out of the seat.

"I'm sorry, I have to get over to the house. I'll text you later," she called over her shoulder as she ran out of the back entrance of the restaurant and then jogged to the house. By the time she slid into the foyer and felt the cool blast of air conditioning, she was soaked in sweat.

"I have to work out more," Juniper said to herself through gasps for air.

"Did you say something?" her cousin Rose asked as she poked her head around the doorframe from the living room. Juniper grabbed the handkerchief from her pocket and wiped her forehead again.

"Forget it. Where is the munchkin?"

Rose pointed to the sofa, where Juniper's daughter Enid was asleep on the sofa. The four-year-old's massive mop of curly brown hair was tied up in a messy ponytail and bound with what looked like a whole roll of glitter ribbon. Even through her exhaustion, Juniper couldn't help but laugh.

"Did you do that to her?"

Rose shook her head and grinned. "I don't even know where she found the ribbon. I was making her lunch and she showed up for her grilled cheese like that. I suggested putting some ribbon back on the roll but she insisted it was magic ribbon and gave her fairy powers. I think the only power it had was knocking her out because she fell asleep right after she ate."

Rose was eighteen and technically Juniper's second cousin, but in the extended Farmer family, no such distinctions were made. Their family was vast and spread out all over different areas of Vermont, though the majority were based in Wintervale or Hadleigh. Juniper's Great-Uncle and Aunt, Steve and Kit Farmer, owned the antique shop in downtown Wintervale, while Rose's family lived in Hadleigh. Rose was taking a gap year between high school and college and offered to be Enid's nanny, an offer Juniper gladly accepted.

"Do you want something to eat?" Rose asked, her voice filled with concern. "I can make you a sandwich in less than a minute. I've timed myself when Enid claims starvation is imminent. My words, not hers."

Juniper laughed as she sat down at the small desk in the hallway. "If my four-year-old starts using SAT words, please let me know. No, I'm fine. I was going to try and catch her before her nap for some playtime, but since she's already down, I'll head up to the stables and clean out the stalls. I also need to get watercress from the greenhouse for tonight's special. Billie called in sick this morning, so I'm short a prep cook."

Rose's face set in a deep scowl.

"Juni, you are doing too much and you know it. You can't keep running this place basically on your own."

Juniper glanced over at the picture sitting next to her on the desk. It was from her wedding and while it was taken only six years ago, it felt like a lifetime had passed without her Danny, the love of her life. He was an emergency room doctor, but they still ran the farm together. On the mornings he didn't have to work, he couldn't wait to wake up and tend to the horses. They would pick apples together in the fall and sell pumpkins at the fall fair in town. Back then, every moment away from him felt like torture. And now...

"I don't need help, Rose. I have you, I have Sebastian. My friends are here when they have the time. I've been doing just fine on my own for four years, haven't I?" she asked as she glanced over at her beautiful, snoring little girl.

Rose smiled sadly. "Is that all you want, Juni? Fine? You and Enid have your whole lives in front of you. You deserve more than just fine."

Juniper's shoulders slumped and she sighed.

"Okay, okay! I will put up an ad for help tonight. But *only* for the stables. I don't need anyone else involved with the farm right now. Will that appease you, Miss Know-It-All Teenager?"

Rose nodded, obviously proud of herself. "It will. Now, do you want to stay here and I can go get the watercress while you take a break?"

Juniper was already on her feet.

"Nope! I'll be home for dinner. Give the munchkin a kiss for me when she wakes up."

"And the ad?" Rose called after her.

"Tonight!" she answered as she ran for the stable. And Juniper knew she had to keep her promise because Rose wouldn't let it go. Then again, maybe she was right...

Everyone needed a little help *sometimes*, right?

Chapter Two

HARLEY

The sun had set in Austin hours ago, though Harley wasn't exactly sure what time it was. All he knew was that it was dark and he couldn't be bothered getting up to turn the lights on. His huge flatscreen TV was casting a blue-ish white pallor over the entire room, but it was bright enough that he could see the empty six pack and cold pizza on the coffee table in front of him. He considered grabbing another sixer of beer from the fridge, but if he couldn't be bothered with the lights, he definitely couldn't summon up the energy to make it to the fridge.

He'd been drinking enough lately that the six beers didn't do much to dull his racing thoughts, and his body was weighed down by a combination of apathy and grief, so he just stayed where he was. Harley spent so much time on that couch, the once sturdy leather had settled into a soft, obvious outline of his body. For the last six weeks, he slept on the couch, he ate on the couch, and he watched the same six shows over and over again on the couch. Only the pizza boy knew him better and even now, the teenager greeted him at the door with an unmistakable grimace of pity.

Maybe I need to order from somewhere else for a while, he thought as he grabbed a piece of cold pepperoni pie from the box in front of him. The canned laughter from the audience on TV just made him more anxious than he already felt, so he switched the channel to a soccer game. Harley wasn't even sure who the teams were but it didn't particularly matter. It was all just white noise since the junkyard fire. He didn't seem to hear anyone when they talked to him now.

Technically, he was supposed to be back at work two weeks ago, but the chief wouldn't clear him for active duty until Harley clocked twelve hours with the department psychiatrist. Since he had no interest in talking to anyone about his problems, it felt like they were locked in a stalemate. How was a therapist going to help him anyway? He'd been knocked unconscious while every member of his company died in a sudden chemical explosion. His best friends, his brothers and sisters, every one of them was gone. The only family he had was gone...

And he'd slept through it.

How was he supposed to forgive himself for that? How was he supposed to go back to a station house filled with strangers? Harley had barely made it through the nine funerals he attended in the weeks following the explosion. Each one was another opportunity to be swept up in grief again, to hold a mother or spouse in his arms who couldn't understand why *their* hero didn't survive, to feel the guilt of being alive. By the time it was all over and the day came where Harley was expected to push his pain away like nothing had happened, he couldn't do it. He just couldn't pretend to be fine; especially when he could hardly get off the sofa.

But he couldn't wallow in his grief... not if he wanted a roof over his head to wallow under, anyway. Harley had been a fire-fighter for his entire adult life, so he didn't think he was qualified for much else. Except there was no way he could go back being a firefighter either. He would have been pretty content to just stay in his hole in the couch forever, but he was running out of savings and he could feel his body reflecting his lifestyle. His beard was also making it clear that he had no one to impress because it was out of control. His whole life was out of control.

No; he couldn't keep living like this. If he wasn't going to go back to the station, he had to find a job. Harley opened his laptop with one eye closed, unsure of whether or not it had enough of a charge left to be of any use.

"Forty percent. That will do it," he said aloud as he pulled up a job search site. The first problem he ran into was his experience. If he was just looking for a transfer to another firehouse, it would have been no problem. But he didn't just want a new job... Harley *needed* an entirely new life. He thought back on his life before he went to the academy, on his life at his grandmother's horse farm. It was the only other life he'd ever known. His Nana Mae actually had to force him to stay in high school, because all he wanted to do was stay home and help with the horses all day.

"Horses," he said thoughtfully as he typed it into the search engine. It was vague, especially because he'd left the options open for the entire country. But he had all night to look and another six pack of beer in the fridge that he suddenly felt the ambition to grab. Once he popped the top on his first, or technically, seventh, beer, he started scrolling through options.

As he suspected, "horses" was a little vague. Most of the jobs that came up were looking for a large animal vet at practices in Montana and Wyoming. Both were beautiful states but they didn't feel far enough away, even when they *did* have a job that fit his meager credentials in the field of horse care. By the time he opened his third, or whatever, beer, he was beginning to lose hope. But then he saw an interesting headline:

Family Farm in Vermont Needs Ranch Hand: Room & Board Inc.

Harley set his beer down on the coffee table and picked up the laptop so he could properly read the ad. His eyebrows seemed to steadily rise higher and higher as he read.

Wintervale Farms in Wintervale, Vermont is in need of a year-round ranch hand. Duties include stable care, large vegetable garden maintenance, and occasional tending of a greenhouse. Salary commensurate to experience, includes a private guest house and meals/food stock. For more information, contact J. Larson via email: owner@wintervalefarms.com

"Huh," he said as he finished off the beer. Vermont was about as far away as he could get from Texas. Harley had grown up in and around Austin, so he'd never seen *real* snowfall once in his whole life. Plus, he could sell his condo, with everything in it, including his Harley shaped couch, and just go. He didn't need much of anything if this place was offering a guest house *and* food. All he needed to do was get in his truck and leave.

Before he lost his nerve, Harley sent a short and to the point email to J. Larson with his resumé attached, then closed the laptop and flopped down in his sleeping position. Apparently, the soccer game had ended at some point and now two guys were shouting at him about sports, so he changed the channel to one that was showing an old movie. He knew it was one of those important "Films" that everyone was meant to have seen by the time they were his age, but he always seemed to miss the beginning.

It looked like he was about to miss the end too, because before he even had a chance to remember the character's names, he was fast asleep. The beer had done its job; it helped him fall asleep. But it wouldn't be long before the nightmares woke him up...

He hoped there might be a response from J. Larson waiting for him when that inevitably happened.

Chapter Three

JUNIPER - ONE MONTH LATER

"**M**iss! Miss! I asked for another glass of sparkling water five minutes ago! Where did our waiter go?"

Juniper bit down on her bottom lip so she didn't lose her cool and end up with a communal table full of one-star reviews on the restaurant's website. She knew for a fact that the woman asked for a refill exactly one minute ago, because Juniper looked at the clock and groaned when she saw how slowly the minutes were passing. Her waiter needed more than sixty seconds to get back to the kitchen, open a new bottle of sparkling water, and come back to the table. But she couldn't say that to the deeply frustrating woman who was currently glaring at her.

"I can see him coming your way right now, miss. And I'll add a piece of our farm-fresh strawberry shortcake to your meal for the trouble."

Before the woman could say anything else, Juniper ran back up to the host stand. She didn't normally take over hosting and manager duties during the day at Wren & Candle, but Sebastian asked if she could cover his shift so he could visit his grandmother in Burlington. Juniper had a hard time saying no to requests involving family. Except he'd neglected to mention the party of twenty that had booked the communal table for lunch. They were staying at The Mountain Wolf Lodge, an upscale resort and living community in Hadleigh, which meant they were going to be just a little bit extra.

Juniper was just about to check on the kitchen before the next reservation arrived, when she saw Rose waving at her from around the side of the barn. And she had Enid in her arms. Juniper's stomach dropped and she cursed under her breath as she snuck away from the host stand and over to her cousin.

"What's going on, Rose? I only have a minute before someone starts yelling at me again."

She didn't even have to ask once she got a look at her little girl, though. Enid's face was pale but her curls were stuck to her forehead with sweat. Her little nose was running and Juniper could hear her whimpering even though Enid had her face buried in Rose's shoulder.

"Did you take her temperature?" Juniper asked as she touched the back of her hand to her daughter's forehead. She was warm, but not burning up.

"Just a tad over a hundred," Rose answered as she shifted the little girl in her arms. "I think it's just a bad cold but I didn't want to make any assumptions without talking to you."

Ever since she lost Danny, Juniper would go into crisis mode if Enid did so much as sneeze. But she knew now wasn't the time to panic. She had to stay calm. She had to...

"Ma'am?"

"WHAT?" she yelled as she spun around to see who was asking anything more of her. When she almost bumped into the giant wall of a man who was standing behind her, she felt her cheeks start to burn. He was taller than her by almost half, and even through his unseasonably warm clothes, Juniper could tell he was muscular. His thick, wavy brown hair was damp from sweat, but for some reason it just made him more handsome. And his eyes...

His eyes.

Juniper couldn't look at anything else.

"I'm sorry, ma'am. If this is a bad time, I can come back later?"

He wasn't wearing a cowboy hat but his accent implied one. Juniper had to shake the stars from her eyes and remember that she was supposed to be working.

"Right, no. I'm sorry I yelled. Can I get you a table? We're booked up until two but there is a private table by the kitchen..."

*What am I doing? Wait... what **was** I doing? Enid! Right. Focus.*

The man smiled kindly, though there was an obvious sadness in his smile.

"No, but thank you, ma'am. I'm Harley Thatcher. We spoke about the ranch hand job? I just got here from Austin."

Juniper was trying to pay attention to what he was saying and not the honeyed, Texas drawl that he was speaking in. It took a few seconds longer than usual for her to put his words together. When she looked behind him, she saw a huge red pick-up parked in the lot.

"Right! Of course. Wait, you drove here from Austin? If you had told me, I could have arranged for hotels on the way."

"It's okay, ma'am. I don't mind sleeping in the truck. Plenty of room."

For a minute, Juniper was frozen as she tried to figure out what she should do next. Everyone in the restaurant was staring at Harley and he had to feel it too. The communal table was just getting their appetizers so they were going to be there for an eternity. Then she heard Enid's croaky little voice behind her call out for her. That was enough to break the spell.

"Right. Rose, can you stay here and watch the restaurant for a few minutes? I'll take Enid back to the house and call you when she's settled in. Harley, why don't you come with me and we can talk at the house?" she asked. He nodded respectfully but Rose was still staring at him. "Rose!"

"Yes," she answered, though Juniper was pretty sure her cousin had no idea what she agreed to. Juniper slipped Enid into her arms and gestured for Rose to go into Wren & Candle. She didn't even have to ask Harley to follow her. He just walked quietly behind her, leaving a few steps between them so he didn't crowd her. It had been a long time since Juniper let a man outside of her family into the farmhouse, so she was mostly trying to regulate her heart beat.

The fact that he took a few steps closer as they walked through the front door didn't help her nerves. She was suddenly super aware of him: his height, how broad shouldered he was, and the scent of him. It was masculine and woodsy, but with just a hint of the summer heat that he'd obviously not expected from Vermont. Juniper turned around to say something to him, anything that might break up this unexpected tension she was feeling in the air between them. In the end, though, she didn't have to do anything.

Because Enid reared back her sweaty little head and sneezed dramatically all over her mother's face.

Chapter Four

HARLEY

Harley had to hide his face behind his sweatshirt's sleeve so Juniper didn't see him laugh when her little girl sneezed right in her face. Her mother barely flinched, but the girl looked like she was going to cry. Her kid was a carbon copy of Juniper, with long thick brown curls and large, curious eyes under eyebrows that made her appear more serious than Harley suspected she was. The only difference was that Enid had eyes the color of the Mediterranian. When they filled with tears, Harley felt like his heart was being ripped out, and he hadn't even done anything to make her cry.

Without missing a beat, Juniper reached down and used Enid's dress to wipe her own face.

"Would you please excuse me for a minute, Harley. I'm going to take her upstairs." It wasn't exactly a question, but he nodded anyway and she disappeared up the stairs. "Help yourself to some of the lemonade in the fridge. There are glasses on the counter!" she called back down to him.

Since he didn't exactly know where the kitchen was, he started down the first hallway he found that led away from the living room. The old farmhouse was a piece of craftsmanship unlike anything Harley had ever seen. It had clearly been built with love a long time ago, because he could tell a lot of the original wood floors and ceiling beams were still in place. It also had the feel of a home that had seen generations of a family grow up inside of it. He loved homes like that. His Nana Mae had a house like that.

As he walked down the hall, he noticed the walls were covered in pictures of, what he assumed, was Juniper's family. There was an old black and white picture of a young couple holding each close at a train station in Perth, Australia. The young man was in a Navy uniform and the girl in his arms was wearing a long floral dress. They looked happy, though the girl's cheeks were streaked with tears. Harley felt that tug on his heart for the second time since he walked in the farmhouse and it was starting to annoy him a little. He'd mostly grown numb to feelings over the last seven months.

There were a handful of other photos, of family holidays, birthdays, and generations of people taken all over the farm. But then Harley noticed a photo of Juniper standing next to a man who wasn't in any other photos. He was handsome in the way an actor from the 1940s was handsome: his jaw was strong, and his smile was reflected in dimples and lines around his eyes. He had the same ocean blue eyes as Enid, but his hair was lighter, long and slicked back behind his ears. The way he looked at Juniper... Even through the photo, Harley could see how much he loved her. And they both glowed with their hands set on Juniper's pregnant tummy.

But that was it. The rest of the pictures were just Juniper and Enid. Harley was still looking at the pictures when Juniper's voice startled him.

"You won't find the lemonade here," she said suddenly, causing him to spin around so fast, he almost fell into the wall.

"No, right, of course not," he stumbled as he tried not to notice the cute summer dress Juniper had changed into. She looked a lot like the young woman in the black and white photo that was taken in Australia. "I was just distracted by that photo of the couple at the train station," he said, hoping the half-truth would keep him out of trouble.

"That's my Great Uncle Steve and Great Aunt Kit. She was an Australian war bride. They own the antique shop in town. If you stop by, they love telling their story. Uncle Steve will even break out his good scotch if you catch him on a nostalgic day. Come on into the kitchen. I'll get you that lemonade and we can talk about the job."

Harley followed Juniper into the kitchen, though he forced himself to look up at the ceiling the whole time, afraid of making her uncomfortable if she caught him staring. And he really wanted to watch her every graceful move. When they got to the kitchen, and he was finally able to look down, he noticed how beautiful, and massive, it was.

"This is a great kitchen. How old is the house?" he asked, hoping some light conversation would distract from the apparent sin he'd just committed by looking at the photos.

Juniper was already pouring the lemonade when he turned around. "The first foundation was built in the mid-1800s. It's been built on to and updated over the years, but a lot of the wood you'll see around is from the original house. I'm sure you're more interested in hearing about the job, though."

Harley laughed awkwardly. "I mean, I can be interested in two things at once."

"Fair enough," she answered as she handed him the glass of ice cold lemonade, which was already sweating from the heat. He was grateful for the lemonade and for the cool touch of her hand when she gave it to him. Juniper gestured for him to sit at the long farm table, then she took the seat across from him, like they were in a boardroom.

"I guess we covered almost everything in the email, but now that you're here, I can give you more details. Just off to the left from the front porch, you'll see the guest house where you'll be living. It's not massive, but it should have everything you need. All the internet info is on the kitchen table in there. Linens are in the bathroom. Your food is covered, too. Daytimes are crazy here, so you'll be on your own. But you're welcome to anything you want from Wren & Candle, or you can eat at the house with us. We have dinner at six every night, mostly to keep Enid on a schedule."

Harley shook his head in surprise. "You were serious about the food part? That's all day, every day?"

Juniper waved her hands around them.

"We live on a farm full of produce. I run a restaurant on the property. Why would I make you buy food when we're surrounded by it? If you order from Wren & Candle, just make sure to give them extra time, because family food comes second to customers. And Rose may be with us for dinner some nights if she's watching Enid."

"I'm such a jerk," Harley said. "Your little girl. Is she okay?"

"I think she just caught a summer cold. She's sleeping right now. Harley, I have to ask you... I don't understand why you're here."

Harley felt like a bucket of cold water had been dumped over him. *Am I about to get fired already?* "I'm afraid I don't follow."

Juniper turned around and grabbed a couple of pieces of paper off the counter. When he saw it was his resumé, his heart sank.

"All of your experience is as a firefighter. I know you said you grew up with horses, and I hired you because I liked the idea of having someone with safety training on the farm. But this job pays nothing compared to what you could be making somewhere else as a firefighter. Why are you in Vermont? Are you running from something and do I need to worry about it?"

Harley almost laughed, but he didn't want to confuse her more. He *was* running from something, but it was something that was going to follow him no matter where he went. He couldn't tell her that, though.

"I just needed a change of scenery, you know? And honestly, I thought the idea of a cool summer would be a change of pace, but obviously," he said as he slipped out of his sweatshirt, "I misjudged that one."

Juniper laughed at him and his stomach did somersaults. She was beautiful when she laughed, but it didn't seem like she did it often.

"Yeah, you did. There is an AC unit in the guest house. You'll have to turn it on when you get in there, because honestly, I forgot you were coming today."

"I'd actually be happy to get right to work, start learning the farm," he said. He felt like he needed to do something physical after being in the truck for so long, but Juniper looked surprised.

"You just got here. Don't you want to settle in?" she asked, looking at her watch.

"I can just drop my stuff off and then do whatever you need while it's still light out." He thought maybe he sounded like an overeager but he was anxious to prove his worth. He wasn't sure why, though.

Juniper looked at her watch again. "Well, the horses need baths and the stalls probably need another quick clean. If you want to acquaint yourself with the ladies and the start on the baths, I'd appreciate it. Then, if you want to eat with us tonight, head back up here a little before six. I'm going to go back to the restaurant, so you can just head out when you're ready."

"That sounds great, ma'am."

She laughed again, softly this time. "As much as I enjoy hearing it in your accent, please, call me Juniper. I don't think I'm ready to be called 'ma'am' yet."

Harley nodded, but right before she shut the door, he called after her, "See you for dinner, Miss Juniper."

The sound of her laugh as she closed the door brought the butterflies back. He didn't expect his new boss to be so fierce and independent. And beautiful.

What had he gotten himself into?

Chapter Five

JUNIPER

Juniper glanced over at the old grandfather clock in the breakfast nook and saw it was almost six. Sebastian had come back earlier than he planned, which meant she was able to get Enid fed before Harley came over. Since her daughter was sick, she got to pick whatever she wanted for dinner. That meant Enid sniffled as she ate a bowl of mac and cheese in front of the TV. One of the waitresses had run over with a bag containing to go containers of the night's specials, along with some cobbler and a pitcher of tea. Juniper was just about to start plating it when there was a knock on the front door.

"MAMA!" Enid yelled in her croaky little voice. "There is a man at the door!"

Juniper quickly tried to shake her hair back into something that resembled a style other than, "sweaty working mother with a sick child" but it was obvious that wasn't going to happen when she caught her reflection in a mirror. Instead, she tried to straighten up her posture a little, then quickly looked around for her shoes, which were suddenly gone. It was taking too long to find them, so she just ran to the front door in her bare feet.

When she opened it, Juniper couldn't help but laugh. Harley

was wearing a tan thermal shirt with the sleeves rolled up all the way and a pair of dark jeans. He was covered in various kinds of dirt from head to toe; even his forehead was streaked with mud. Juniper hoped it was mud anyway. As she continued to try and stifle her laughter, Harley put his hands on his hips.

"You didn't warn me that *the ladies* weren't overly fond of strangers," he said, his accent a little heavier because he was frustrated. "If I hadn't ducked, the piebald would have kicked me right in the chest!"

Juniper cringed. "Okay, *that* I do feel bad about. Maiden isn't overly fond of men. She came to us as an abused foal, so it takes time to earn her trust. We can talk about it over dinner."

Harley looked down at his clothes, all the way down to his boots, then back up to his hands.

"I don't want you to delay dinner on my account, Miss Juniper, especially if the little one needs to eat," he said as he glanced over at Enid, who was bundled up in a blanket watching her favorite princess movie. Juniper was loaded up to argue with him about calling her "miss" too, but she had a feeling there were only so many arguments like that she would win with him.

"Enid already ate, so why don't you go get cleaned up and come back when you're done? It's from the restaurant tonight so it will reheat."

"Are you sure..."

She waved him off the porch. "Go ahead. I'll be here when you get back."

Harley gave her another polite tip of the head, the kind that made it seem like he was missing a cowboy hat, then walked briskly off in the direction of the guest house. When Juniper shut the door, she turned around to find Enid staring at her.

"What's the matter, baby?"

Enid wiped her nose on her pajama sleeve. "Nothing. But your face is red. Do you have a fever too, mommy?"

Juniper chuckled, then walked over so she could give Enid a kiss on the top of her head.

"I'm just fine, moppet. I'm going to set the table for dinner and when Harley gets back, you can have a proper introduction. Does that sound good?"

Enid nodded, instead hypnotised by a song in the movie that they had listened to about a thousand times between car rides and princess play time. Juniper took it as her cue to head back to the kitchen. Since she didn't know how long it would take him to clean up, she left the food in the boxes and instead focused on setting the small table in the breakfast nook. She also tried to figure out why she was so nervous. He was just another guy who worked at the farm. At any given time, there were a half dozen of them or more. Why was she suddenly acting all silly about *this* guy?

As soon as she let her mind drift a little too far into the question, she happened to glance over at the picture of her with Danny that hung on the wall. It was their last picture together before he went to work at the hospital one night and, in the middle of treating a patient, crumpled to the floor. They told her it was an aneurism. They promised that he never felt a thing. Juniper was sure their baby heard the news too, because Enid went from her usual kick-boxing sessions in her mother's stomach to complete stillness. It was just for a moment, but Juniper was sure even Danny's unborn daughter felt the loss of her daddy. The light he brought to a room was gone, and in all the years since, she still felt its absence so keenly.

And then Harley walked up to her.

He was so different from Danny, but he had that same light in his eyes, even if it was clouded over by a sort of sadness. Was that what scared her? The idea of being around that kind of brightness again?

She didn't have time to think about it anymore because Enid yelled, "MOMMY! Door!" again. Juniper looked up at the clock and saw half an hour had passed.

How long have I been setting the table?

Juniper wiped a tear from her cheek and gently touched the picture of Danny as she walked by, like she always did every time she passed it. This time, though, she took a deep breath and tried to put the past out of her mind. If Harley saw his new boss crying on his first night at the farm, he'd probably get in his truck and drive back to Texas.

She wouldn't have blamed him if he did.

Chapter Six

HARLEY

Harley rushed as fast has he could manage to get ready, but he still felt like he took forever, and he hated that he was leaving Juniper waiting. After a quick shower, he put on his last remaining pair of clean jeans, a t-shirt, and a flannel, slipped into his boots, then jumped out the door, tying the laces as he went. His hair was still wet when he got to the farmhouse but he figured it was better than being even later to dinner.

When Juniper opened the door for him, nothing had changed, except now Enid was drinking a milkshake, which Harley assumed was made with homemade ice cream. This time, Enid waved at him when he came into the house.

"Hi, Mr. Harley, sir. Mama said I have to be extra nice. You can have some of my ice cream!" Her throat must have been sore because she sounded like a little frog. Harley gave her a little bow.

"That's a generous offer, Miss Enid, and it does look delicious. But that looks like it was made special, just for you. Perhaps another time, we can share a banana split?"

Enid's eyes got wide.

"Mama! What is a banana split?"

Harley winced and Juniper stifled a laugh behind her hand.

"Thanks for that. Enid, the next time you see Uncle Steve, you ask him that question. I guarantee you will have a banana split before you know it. Alright, moppet, this is your last movie and then you're going to bed. Deal?"

Enid didn't answer; she was already deeply invested in an animated movie that came out long before Harley was even born. He was impressed by the little girl's taste in films.

"I just reheated everything in the oven. I'm sure you want to eat and get to sleep. It's been a long day," Juniper said as he followed her through the picture hallway and back to the breakfast nook. The table had already been set and the plates were covered with cloches, which Juniper pulled away before they sat down. When Harley saw the feast in front of him, he actually chuckled at the memory of his last meal: a bag of tortilla chips and a package of cheese he'd grabbed at a gas station.

"I don't mean to laugh," he said when he noticed Juniper looking at him strangely as they sat down. "I was just trying to remember the last time I had a home cooked meal."

"Well, this was technically cooked by my chefs, but we try to make it feel homey. This is our lemon-salted roasted salmon with a rum sweet potato purée and caramelized Brussel sprouts. We usually put the sweet potato with another dish but we had kind of a bumper crop of sweet potatoes this year. If you want a basket, just let me know."

This time, Harley laughed out loud. "I wouldn't know what to with a sweet potato if there was money riding on it."

"Really? I thought firemen were supposed to be amazing cooks."

Harley tried not to let his expression change. "Only one or two of us has to be. The rest just reap the benefits."

He hoped she would change the subject. He knew he had a tendency to go dark on people when the firehouse came up and the last thing Harley wanted to do was ruin this nice meal she'd put together for him. He was grateful when she changed the subject back to food.

"I'm lucky I have generations of family recipes to fall back on. Some of our biggest sellers are based on the recipes Aunt Kit brought with her from Australia. Wait until pumpkin season. Our pumpkin soup is the best in the world."

Harley couldn't help but notice the way she lit up when she talked about her family. And food. She was so passionate about both that her eyes sparkled when she talked about them. He forgot what it was like to be that excited about *anything*, but there was something about this farm...

He was already starting to remember what it felt like.

"Harley?"

Oh, crap. He hadn't been listening to her. Just staring.

"I'm sorry, what did you say?"

She raised her eyebrow. "I asked if your family was originally from Texas."

"Ah. Right. No family to speak of, miss. I had a grandmother but she passed right before..."

Right before the only other family I had died in an explosion.

He couldn't bring himself to say the words out loud. They lingered at the back of his throat, as if he was actually desperate to tell her. But he still couldn't talk about it. He just... couldn't.

"I'm sorry to hear that, Harley. But I'm sure Enid and Rose would agree with me if I said you should consider yourself a part of our family. She doesn't just offer to share her ice cream with anyone," Juniper said with a wink. Somehow, that was all Harley needed to bring him back from that dark place. For the moment anyway.

"Would it be rude of me to ask how it ended up just you and Enid in this big old house?" he asked before he finally took a bite of his delicious food. Harley was glad he'd asked a question because he wanted to savor the taste of the salmon. Juniper took a long, deliberate sip of her iced tea before she answered him.

"It was mom and dad's house before me. They passed on around the same time, and I was the only kid, so the Farm became my responsibility. Enid's dad and I lived here for about two years, then it's been Enid and me for the last four. It's a big house but luckily we have a large group of family and friends with virtually *no* boundaries, so we're never lacking in visitors."

Harley laughed a little more loudly than he intended to. Juniper was funny, but she didn't act like she was, which only made her more funny. It was an impressive balance. He also appreciated the careful way she kept her secrets while still telling him the truth. He admired that skill a lot.

They ended up chatting for about an hour before Harley yawned so loudly, it automatically caused Juniper to yawn too.

"I guess it really *has* been a long day," Harley said with a laugh as he stretched. "I should head back."

He helped Juniper load all of the dishes into the dishwasher and then she followed him out to the front door. At some point while they were eating, Enid had fallen fast asleep on the couch, snuggled up with her blanket and a soft doll with bright pink hair. Juniper walked over and managed to pick up Enid, the blanket, and the doll in one swift movement without waking her daughter up. They didn't speak, but Juniper smiled at him, and he nodded back his thanks for dinner. Before he fully shut the door behind him, he glanced back to watch as she carried Enid up the stairs to her bedroom. As he watched her, so fierce but yet, so loving, he had to force himself to turn and quietly close the door behind him.

As he walked back to the guest house, *his* house, he kept telling himself that he couldn't get attached. Nothing was permanent. And he couldn't fall in love with another family...

Just to lose them all over again.

Chapter Seven

JUNIPER

"I can't believe you didn't bring our moppet with you! We haven't seen enough of either of you lately."

Juniper spun around in an old barbershop chair that had been sitting in her Aunt and Uncle's antique shop for years. It was one of those things that her Uncle Steve thought was going to sell as soon as they put a price tag on it. Instead, eight years later, it was mostly something for Enid to play on whenever she came to Golden Oldies with her mom.

"I'm sorry, Aunt Kit," Juniper answered after she spun in another circle. "But she has a really bad cold and I left the house too early to try and coax her off the couch. Anyway, Rose is with her. They were watching cartoons and eating ice pops when I left, so I wasn't going to convince her to leave."

When Juniper woke up earlier that morning, she had a text from her Aunt Kit. They'd bought an old wall hanging and they thought it would be perfect for Wren & Candle. It was made of iron, twisted and turned into a sort of floral shape, and covered in tealight candle holders. Her Aunt was right; Juniper knew the exact place in the restaurant to put it the moment she saw the picture. Rose didn't usually watch Enid on the weekends, but

Juniper was covering Saturday lunch. She had just enough time to go to Golden Oldies, chat with her Aunt and Uncle for a bit, and make it back for the brunch crowd.

Kit was dusting off the antiques in the shop, quickly brushing the feather duster over Juniper's face as she walked by, which made her sneeze.

"So, who is this new fella you have working at the farm?" Kit asked. Juniper couldn't help but laugh. She'd never even told them about Harley.

"He's been in Wintervale for *one whole day*. How did his arrival already make it down the Green Mountain Granny gossip pipeline?" she asked, invoking the name of her Aunt's exercise and travel group. All of the older ladies in town got together once a week for exercise, coffee, and conversation about what was going down in Wintervale. More than once, the women's ability to convince people to spill their life stories had aided the police in solving crimes. Juniper only hoped she had half of her Aunt Kit's energy if she made it to 92.

But the gossiping... it could be really exhausting.

"Honey," Kit said as she sat down in a plump old armchair next to Juniper, "when a proper cowboy from Texas shows up in Wintervale, *everyone* is going to hear about it. And you know it."

Juniper laughed. "Technically, he's a firefighter. And he worked with horses, not cows. We don't even have cows on the farm."

"Does he wear the hat?" Steve asked, poking his head up from behind the counter.

"No hat," Juniper said, rolling her eyes. "But he does have the accent. And he's ridiculously polite. I practically had to beg him to stop calling me 'ma'am.' He also seems kind of sad and maybe a little lonely? I don't know. He just got here. We've had one conversation. It was nice, though..." she felt herself trail off and when she looked back up, her Aunt and Uncle were grinning at her. "What?" she asked.

"You like him," Kit answered with a grin.

"I don't... I mean... we met yesterday! He seems like a good guy, and I wouldn't have hired him to work at my home if I didn't trust him, but he's been in Wintervale less than twenty-four hours. I'd prefer it if you two didn't get any ideas."

They held their hands up defensively, in unison, which made Juniper laugh. It was amazing how in sync a couple got after over seventy years together.

"I didn't say anything," Steve answered quickly. "I just think your parents would be pretty impressed that you hired a cowboy to work on Wintervale Farms. We Farmers are a lot of things, but cowboys isn't one of them."

"I seriously don't think he'd consider himself a cowboy. And either way, I think mom and dad would have been more impressed if I figured out how to manage the farm on my own. They didn't need to hire help when it came to the horses and the other day-to-day stuff I'm finding it impossible to keep up with," Juniper said before letting out a long sigh. She tried not to think about it too often, but without Danny, and without her parents, she was lonely sometimes too.

Kit reached out and took Juniper's hand in her own. "You listen to me, young lady. Your parents ran the farm *together*. You and Danny ran the farm *together*. And now you are trying to do it all on your own with a child and very popular restaurant. Do you think I could keep up with all the nonsense in this shop without your Uncle? There are a lot of things that you do on your own and you're amazing at them. You are a wonderful mother, Juni. Wren & Candle was *your* idea and you started it all by yourself. But it is completely reasonable to need help when you are already shouldering so much on your own. I only wish we could help you more."

Juniper squeezed her Aunt's hand.

"You both help me more than you ever could imagine. Enid and I would be lost without you."

While they were talking, Steve had disappeared into the back of the store and returned carrying the obviously heavy wall hanging they'd bought for her. He was 94-years-old and still hauling around antiques like a man in his twenties.

"We aren't going anywhere anytime soon, Juni, except out to your truck, because this thing is a monster!" Steve said, hoisting the decoration up on his shoulder. Juniper jumped to her feet and opened the front door for him, saying a quick goodbye to her Aunt before she chased her uncle out to the truck they used to haul stuff around for the farm. Steve hoisted it into the back and set it down gently, even though Juniper could see him put his back into it.

"I could have helped, Uncle Steve!" she said as she ran up behind him. He pretended to wipe sweat from his forehead and laughed.

"I can handle it, baby girl. And you listen to me. I may just be your old-as-the-mountains uncle, but I hope you know how proud of you we are. Aunt Kit was telling the truth in there. I don't care if this new fella is a cowboy or not. I'm just glad you are finally getting some help out there. If things kept staying as busy as they are, I was going to volunteer to muck out the stalls on the weekend."

Juniper laughed, but it wasn't doing much to hide the tears in her eyes. She really did love her Great Aunt and Uncle so much. If her parents were happy about anything in the hereafter, it was that Steve and Kit cared about their daughter and granddaughter so much, and watched over them so well.

"Hey, why don't you two come over for dinner tomorrow night? I can make the chicken Aunt Kit likes, you can see Enid, and I'll invite Harley so you get a chance to meet him properly."

Steve pulled Juniper into a tight hug. "We'll be there with bells on. Just let us know what time. And I may have something new for Enid's robot collection."

"Oh, gosh, are you sure?" Juniper said as she pictured all of the shelves in Enid's room covered in vintage robot toys. For some reason, Enid loved them, and her Great-Great Uncle was going to keep her stocked until the end of time.

"I'm sure" he answered when he finally let her go. "And this one is a doozy."

She couldn't even be annoyed with him. The truth was, she'd probably give Enid a second room in the house to store her collection if she wanted. It was a special tradition that had become part of their family. And Juniper knew better than most...

Family, no matter if it's the one you're born into or the one you make for yourself, is more important than anything else in the world.

Chapter Eight

HARLEY

Harley had gotten so used to sleeping on his lumpy old couch, he was actually having a hard time getting comfortable on the amazing mattress in the guest house. Since he was waking up before the sunrise most mornings, he usually just got dressed and started his work. Even though it was Sunday, there was still work to be done in the stable, and 4am was as good a time to get moving as any. Harley put on his jeans and t-shirt, then his boots, and walked out into the unexpectedly humid pre-dawn air.

"I should have looked up the weather before I moved here," he said as he stripped off the t-shirt and tossed it on a chair on the porch. It was early enough that no one was going to be awake, so he wasn't particularly worried about his modesty. Plus, it was better to muck out the stalls before the sun came up, because Juniper had six horses and they didn't seem interested in cleaning up after themselves.

He started in the palomino, Magic's, stall. She was the youngest of the horses and in a few years, was going to be Enid's. All of them were part of a horse therapy group that the farm sponsored on the weekends during the school year. They also had horse camp in the summer, which Harley was actually looking forward to. He actually laughed quietly to himself at the thought. Even before the accident, he couldn't imagine himself being stoked over the idea of hanging out with kids.

Every time his mind was occupied by something that was muscle memory, like shoveling out stalls, it would drift to his friends, or his grandmother. This morning, he couldn't stop thinking about his Nana Mae. Harley never knew either of his parents. In fact, he barely knew anything about them at all. All he knew was that from as far back as he could remember, his nana was the only family he had. His circle may have expanded when he became a firefighter, but Nana Mae raised him, she supported him through some tough high school years where he rebelled against nothing in particular, and cheered for him when he rocked the firefighters exam.

So, when she passed away, Harley thought it was the worst thing that could ever happen to him. She'd been the most important person in his life for so long, and without her...

"Woah, there, cowboy!"

Harley lost control of the shovel on the backswing and spun around to find it in Juniper's hands.

Oh, my god, I almost hit her in the head with a shovel.

"Juniper, uh... good reflexes. I'm so sorry! I didn't know you were back there!" He looked up and saw the sun had risen. *How long have I been in here?*

"It's fine," she said as she handed the shovel back. "I grew up on a farm. I've had a lot worse than a shovel thrown at my head. How long have you been in here?" she asked, scanning the stalls to see that five out of six were almost spotless... as spotless as a horse stall can be, anyway.

Harley laughed awkwardly. "What time is it?" Juniper looked at her watch.

"It's just after seven."

"A while. I've been in here a while."

She gave Maiden a nuzzle on the nose and peeked into her stall. "I'd say so. You must have been up before the rooster."

"You have a rooster?"

Juniper smiled. "Somewhere around here. There is a chicken coop behind the farmhouse but Enid is in charge of that usually. She wanted a chore to help the restaurant and she only drops five or six eggs a week, so I'm not going to tell her no. Speaking of, she is still asleep and Rose is already up there. I have to get ready for the Sunday brunch crowd. If you want something to eat, come by the restaurant around nine? I can save you a plate."

For some reason, Harley couldn't force himself to speak. Not in normal human words anyway.

"No. I mean, yes. Of course. A plate would be... delicious?"

*Did I hit **myself** in the head with a shovel?*

Juniper looked at him with the appropriate amount of suspicion. He sounded like a crazy person. She nodded at him and started to walk out of the barn, then paused for a second and spun back around.

"I almost forgot. My Uncle Steve and Aunt Kit are coming over for dinner tonight. Wren & Candle is closed Sunday nights, so we do family dinner at the house. Steve, Kit, and Rose will be there. Her parents are on a cruise to Hawaii or else they'd come too. My friends Frannie and Micah may join, as long as he doesn't get held up at the church."

"Church?" Harley asked.

"He's the pastor at Wintervale Fellowship. They are opposites in every way and probably two of the most perfectly suited people I've ever met. You'll really like them. If you want to come, of course."

Harley froze up for a second. Even when he was with his Nana Mae, they didn't really have family dinners. They would eat in front of the TV when he was a kid. When he got older, she'd leave a plate for him in the fridge and he'd eat alone in his room. At the firehouse, they all ate dinner together, but the idea of being in that situation again... it made his heart beat a little too fast, like he was going to be sick all over the floor of the barn.

Juniper was staring at him, waiting for an answer, and he didn't know what to say. Why did he get like this when she was around? He must have looked like a real goofball. He couldn't possibly say no. What reason would he have? There wasn't any. In fact, as he watched her standing there in a sundress, with the pink morning sky glittering off her hair, he would have been willing to agree to almost anything. Harley had to take a deep breath before he answered, just so he didn't embarrass himself by shouting his answer and scaring the horses.

"Yes," he said quickly, in an attempt to keep it simple. "I would like to come to your family dinner. Thank you for inviting me."

Now I just sound like a robot, he thought in irritation.

She smiled at him again, that same smile that seemed to make her cheeks glow in rose gold. "Great. Just head up around 6:30. It's super casual so no worries about dressing up. A shirt might not hurt, though."

Harley felt his stomach drop as he looked down at his bare torso, covered in sweat, mud, and random bits of hay. He was going to apologize but before he could say anything, Juniper was already walking away. He didn't know what it was about her, but whenever she was around, he seemed to lose what little sense of control he felt like he had left.

You've got to get it together, buddy, the voice in his head chastised. *Get it together before you do something silly, like fall in love*. A month ago, complications like Juniper were the last thing he wanted. But now...

Chapter Nine

JUNIPER

The farmhouse kitchen was filled with the smells of beer can chickens on the grill outside coming through the windows, and smashed potatoes and cheesy garlic asparagus roasting in the oven. Kit was making a salad at the counter while Juniper and Rose set the big table in the dining room. Normally, on a warm, clear night like tonight, they would eat at the big farm table on the deck, but since Enid still wasn't feeling well, they decided to stay inside. Enid loved to help set the table, but Juniper suspected her daughter was perfectly content tonight in the living room with her Uncle Steve and Harley, who were both lavishing her with attention.

At the last minute, Micah got a dinner invite from an elderly parishioner and he felt obligated to oblige, so he and Frannie weren't going to make it. That meant it was just the family and Harley, and at first, Juniper worried that he might feel outnumbered by them. Instead, he showed up in a nice button down shirt and a pair of khakis, even though she told him not to dress up. As soon as he walked through the door, her Uncle Steve shook his hand like they were old friends, then invited Harley to join him and Enid on the couch for a story.

Tonight, it was about the time Steve broke both of his arms in an accident right *after* the war was over. He always followed the story up by picking Enid up to prove how strong he was now, so Juniper looked forward to the sound of her inevitable giggles. She must have let her mind wander off because when she looked up, Rose was smiling at her.

"What? Why is *everyone* looking at me like that lately?" she asked as she slammed a fork down on the table with enough force to make the whole table shimmy. Juniper flinched at her overreaction and looked around the corner into the living room to make sure Enid hadn't heard. Instead, she was enthralled as Uncle Steve used his hands to mimic war planes flying through the sky. At this rate, her daughter was going to try and join the Navy by the time she was twelve.

Juniper turned back around and saw that Rose was still smiling at her.

"Just say it, please."

Rose shrugged. "You just look happy. That's all. It's not a bad thing, Juni."

"I'd be happier if you put the fork on the left side of the plate, where it belongs."

Rose rolled her eyes.

"Stop deflecting. You are *allowed* to be happy."

Why does everyone keep saying that to me? Juniper thought with frustration.

"I'm not... I don't... I... can you please just go check on the chicken? I'll finish up here. And grab the salad dressing when you come back through please."

Once Rose was gone, Juniper put her hands on the back of a chair and leaned forward as she tried to gain some sense of control again. It had been two days and already, Harley was spinning her world upside down. He wasn't doing anything... not intentionally, anyway. But there was something about his mere presence in Wintervale that made her feel like everything was topsy-turvy.

Juniper closed her eyes and took a few slow, deep breaths. When she heard the sound of the salad dressing being set down on the table, she let out one last long sigh.

"Thanks, love," she said.

"Uh... no problem, honey?" answered a voice that was *not* Rose's. Juniper looked up and was so caught off guard, her hands slipped down the sides of the chair and she almost fell forward into the table. Harley reached out to grab her, but she quickly regained control of her balance and shook off the feeling of falling.

"I'm sorry. I thought you were Rose."

He half-grinned at her. "I hear that a lot."

Juniper laughed as she brushed her hair out of her eyes. "Can I get you anything?"

"I thought I'd see if you needed any help. Well, Steve sent me in here to see if you needed help. Apparently, his next story might not be appropriate for me?"

Juniper set the last glass down on the table and headed for the kitchen. "He's going to read Enid a kid's book about robots from the 50s. It's one of their special traditions. I don't understand it and I don't ask questions."

Harley laughed as he followed behind her.

"Fair enough, miss. *Is* there anything I can help you with?" he asked, his politeness giving Juniper a case of jelly legs.

"Yeah, you can stop calling me 'miss.' I promise, I will not be offended if you call me by my name. Also, Rose is waving her arms from the porch, so I think the chicken is ready. Can you go put them on the platter and bring them to table, please?"

Harley nodded wordlessly and disappeared outside just long enough for Juniper to catch her Aunt grinning at her too. The look on Juniper's face must have been enough to cool Kit down because she pretended to zip her lips and carried the salad into the dining room. Soon, they were all gathered around the dining room table, with Enid in her booster seat. Steve sliced up the aromatic chicken as everyone else passed plates around for sides. For the first time in a *very* long time, the dining room table felt full, it felt complete, and Juniper tried to tell her heart to stop beating so fast.

"So, Harley," Steve started once the chicken was passed around, "I hear you were a firefighter once upon a time."

Juniper saw Harley's face go pale, but he nodded with a gentle smile.

"I was, sir. For six years. It took me a few years of rambling around to figure out what I wanted to do, but then my Nana Mae kicked my..." he paused to censor himself in Enid's presence and Juniper had to hide a laugh behind her napkin. "Nana Mae finally helped me find some direction. It was the best six years of my life."

Steve finished chewing and nodded thoughtfully. "What brought you to our little corner of the world then?"

Juniper, Rose, and Kit all leaned forward at the same time. *Maybe he was about to finally open up*, Juniper thought as she watched him carefully. It seemed like he was almost on the verge of saying it, of telling the truth, but then he took a long, deliberate sip of his ice tea and shrugged a little dismissively.

"I've never lived anywhere but Texas. Sometimes you just need a change of scenery, you know?"

Juniper, Rose, and Kit all sank back into their chairs with noticeable disappointment. Juniper was sure that Harley noticed, because he almost smiled at her, but stopped short. The conversation moved on to other topics, like the farm, the horse camp, and the craziness of Christmas in Wintervale, before Enid let out a long yawn.

"Mama, can we have cake? I'm sleepy," she asked with a sniffle.

"Oh, yes! I made a strawberry pound cake!" Kit reminded everyone, which was unnecessary since Enid had clearly been thinking about it since Kit and Steve got there. Harley looked at his watch and let out a little sigh.

"I would love to stay for dessert, but I am stuffed. Plus, it's going to be a hot one tomorrow and I want to do some weeding in the garden before the sun gets too high. Can I help clean up or anything?"

Everyone started objecting at the same time, which made Harley laugh.

"I'll bring some leftovers and a piece of cake over tomorrow," Juniper said before he left. He thanked her again before he left and said goodnight with a tip of a hat he wasn't wearing. Once he was gone, Kit let out a huff of air like she'd been holding her breath for hours.

"That boy is a *looker!*" she said as she fanned herself off with her napkin. Juniper dropped her head into her hands and groaned as Steve and Rose laughed.

Enid suddenly let out a little cough to clear her throat so she could talk.

"Mama... what does Harley look at?"

Juniper looked at her Aunt with daggers.

"The horses, moppet. Harley likes to look at the horses."

Juniper was suddenly really glad her daughter was still at an age where she accepted explanations without too many questions. She had a hard enough time understanding her *own* feelings about Harley. The last thing she wanted was her daughter getting too attached to a man who might have no intention of staying in Wintervale for longer than the summer.

Now she just needed to remind herself not to get attached either, and it was already proving harder than she expected...

Chapter Ten

HARLEY

The sun was just starting to rise as Harley walked out onto his porch. He had slept in longer than he meant to, because it had been a long night filled with nightmares which meant he woke up constantly. He wanted to be in the garden before it got hot, but now he was going to work at the hottest time of day. Harley had just shut the door behind him when he heard the sound of someone running up the hill behind him. He knew it was Juniper before she said anything; her shampoo smelled like lavender and a hint of it was on the wind.

"Harley, wait," she said, out of breath. "I need to ask you a huge favor."

He turned around and was surprised to see Juniper in her pajamas, her hair still wet from a shower.

"You can ask."

She brushed her hair out of her eyes with a tired sigh. "Rose just called. She caught Enid's cold but because of her asthma, it's a lot worse for her. Normally, I would just bring Enid up to Wren & Candle with me, but she doesn't feel good either. I haven't figured out what to do yet, but would you be able to sit with her for a few hours until I find a friend who can come over? I just need to finish getting ready, get the specials for the day sorted out, and then I can start making calls. I promise it won't be for long."

Juniper was obviously desperate, but Harley's only experience with kids was helping them at fires. He could entertain a scared little kid until they went to the hospital or until their parents were with them, but hours of being alone with a little girl? He wasn't sure he was cut out for babysitting.

She must have sensed his hesitation.

"I swear. She's barely even awake. Her breakfast is in the fridge and she can get it herself. All you have to do is sit there and watch a cartoon with her until I find someone to come take your place. *Please*?" she pleaded. Harley felt like he couldn't say no to her, though he wasn't sure why.

"Okay, for a little while. But as soon as you find someone, you should send them over. I don't know if kids really like me or not," he said nervously. She grabbed his arm and pulled him toward the house, shaking her head furiously.

"I'm sure you're great! You were a fireman, right?" By the time they got in the house, Enid was already snuggled up on the couch with her blanket, and eating from a pre-prepared yogurt parfait. Before Harley even knew what was happening, Juniper had changed, run out the door, and left Harley standing in the living room. He wasn't quite sure what to do at first, because it didn't seem like Enid was even aware of him. Then, she pulled her blanket closer to her and patted the cushion on the other side of the sofa.

"Sit," she said through a mouthful of granola. "Mama said I can watch TV again since I'm sick."

Harley approached her, nervously at first. But when she looked up at him with those stunning blue eyes and her little red nose, he couldn't say no to her. He sat down next to her on the couch and tried to catch up on whatever she was watching, but it seemed to involve a princess who could do magic. Harley was just about to ask her about the show when Enid got up from under her blanket and disappeared into the kitchen. A few minutes later, she came back with two cups and handed him a plastic tumbler full of pink liquid.

"What is this, Enid?" he asked hesitantly.

"Strawberry milk. Mama makes it from real strawberries for me. You can have some."

He tried not to laugh at the thought of anyone finding him drinking strawberry milk from a sippy cup, but he didn't want to hurt Enid's feelings either. Harley couldn't remember the last time he had strawberry milk, but he was probably Enid's age and it was definitely the cheap stuff from a can. With one eye closed nervously, he took a quick sip from the short straw and...

It was good.

No; it was actually great. It wasn't too sweet, it wasn't too rich, and there was just a hint of another flavor in it... maybe mint? If the tiny straw hadn't been acting as a barrier, he might have chugged it all down in one gulp.

"Enid, does your mom serve this in the restaurant?"

She nodded as she took another sip. "There is a grownup version that I can't have. This is *my* special recipe. Mama said the kids get my recipe."

Harley nodded knowingly and made a mental note to check out the grownup version the next time he went over to Wren & Candle. Once they'd talked about her milk, suddenly Enid was telling him about the show, her robot collection, her friends at pre-school... and then, her daddy.

"He went to heaven when I was still in mama's tummy. But lots of times I still say good morning and goodnight to him. Mama says he would like that."

"Heaven, huh?" Harley had expected as much, but it was sadder hearing it from Enid. "And that's a picture of him in the hallway?"

She craned her little neck around the corner. "Yes, that is

daddy. I have his picture in my room. Mama said he was at work, helping people. That was his job. And he got very very sick. She says he misses me a lot. Right, mama?"

Harley looked up and Juniper was staring at them both, with her arms crossed over her chest, as she tapped her foot. She didn't look angry, per say. Just a little surprised.

"Yes, baby. That's right. Harley, my friend Frannie is going to come watch Enid as soon as she's done with her morning meeting. I can stay until she gets here, so if you want to go back to work."

Harley didn't know why, but he jumped to his feet, said a quick goodbye over his shoulder to Enid and ran out the door.

"Thank you!" Juniper called after him, but he was already half-way to the gardens by then. Once he was hidden inside of the rows of tomato plants, he began picking the ripest ones furiously, like he was being paid by the tomato. He had no idea why he reacted the way he did. Was it because Enid told him the whole truth about her father? Was it because Juniper seemed a little annoyed that he knew? Or was it just because Juniper and Enid Larson were slowly letting him into their family?

Harley had no idea what was going on inside of his head, but before he even realized it, he'd not only weeded the entire garden, but filled two baskets full of fresh produce. When he looked up at the sun, he realized it had to be noon, or close to it. There was an unfamiliar car parked outside of the farmhouse, so Juniper's friend must have arrived. He wasn't sure he could face Juniper again, not yet. Instead, he hauled the two baskets of fruit and vegetables up to the back door of Wren & Candle, knocked on the door as loudly as he was able, then hightailed it toward the stable to start working with the horses.

While he was aware of what he was doing, he still couldn't believe he was doing it.

Why are you acting like a teenager, Harley Thatcher? You're embarrassing yourself, he thought as he stopped at the door to the stable. He felt even sillier as he watched Juniper open the door, see the baskets, and then look around for him, just to find he'd run off the second he left them.

Even seventeen-year-old Harley was embarrassed for him right now.

Chapter Eleven

JUNIPER

It was a humid night, there wasn't a cloud in the sky, and for some reason, Juniper couldn't sleep. She wasn't even tired, which was unusual after a busy day at the restaurant. Even though it was Sebastian's week to cover the dinner shift and closing, the lunch shift had been exhausting, and she felt like she couldn't stop moving the rest of the night. Juniper didn't even bother trying to sleep. She tried reading for a while, but she kept reading the same sentence over and over again. If she turned on the TV, it would wake up Enid immediately. She had some sort of super sense when it came to the television and would sleepwalk in the direction of even the slightest noise.

Juniper gave up around midnight, grabbed her robe off the back of her bedroom door, and crept quietly down the stairs. Once she was out on the porch, the unexpectedly cool night air seemed to relax her as she curled up on the porch swing. It was as quiet as a summer night could get on the farm; the crickets were chirping, one of the chickens was clucking softly from the coop, and an owl was hooting in the distance. Juniper closed her eyes and took a long deep breath. She was actually starting to feel a little bit calmer.

And then she heard a blood curdling scream come from the guest house.

Her mom instincts immediately kicked in and Juniper ran across the front yard and to the house in her bare feet, her robe blowing out behind her. When she got to the door, she found it unlocked and slid inside. There were no lights on, but the moonlight through the window made it just bright enough that she could see Harley sitting on the edge of the bed with his head in his hands.

"Harley, I'm going to turn the lights on, okay," she said in the soothing voice she saved for Enid after she had a nightmare. "Tell me it's okay."

He didn't say anything but she could see him nod his head in the dark. When Juniper clicked on the light, Harley was in his pajama pants, but wearing no top. Even though the AC was humming away in the window, he was soaked in sweat, like he'd just finished running a marathon. Juniper crossed over to him and sat down on the very edge of the bed, making sure he had space to breathe.

"Nightmare?" she asked in a whisper. He nodded again.

"Apparently it's called a 'night terror.' According to the internet, anyway."

Juniper let the moment sit as he took deep breaths, like he was trying to regulate his heartbeat. She tried not to look at him as he swept his damp hair away from his forehead and laughed, almost bitterly.

"I thought maybe they would stop when I moved out here. It's so quiet at night. But I think the quiet makes them worse."

As much as she wanted to know what he was dreaming about, Juniper knew it wasn't her place to push him. She also felt a little guilty because she couldn't stop glancing at him out of the corner of her eye. She forced herself into mom mode again.

"Why don't I make you some hot chocolate? I'm pretty sure I got you some chocolate bars from the shop in town," Juniper said as she jumped to her feet and ran over to the kitchen. She opened the fridge and took out a cold bottle of milk that came from a farm over in Hadleigh, added a few pieces of the chocolate, then got both simmering gently on the stove.

"I didn't even look in the fridge or the cabinets. I had no idea any of that was there."

Juniper looked back at him in surprise. "What have you been drinking?"

"Water from the tap. Once I found the glasses, I just kind of stopped there. You've been so generous with meals and during the day I just..."

Juniper turned back from the stove with her eyebrow raised, which made Harley laugh, for real this time.

"I just grab a tomato from the garden or something to hold me over until dinner. I hope that's okay."

She had no idea how to answer him. The question was almost ridiculous; *of course*, she didn't care if he ate fruit and veggies from the garden. But she didn't want to upset him or say anything he might misconstrue, given the state she found him in.

"Harley, you can have whatever you want here. I told you to make yourself at home," Juniper said as she stirred the cocoa. She opened the spice cabinet, poured in a touch of vanilla extract, then filled the mug she'd set aside before she started. When she handed it to him, he shook his head in surprise.

"You just made me hot cocoa from scratch and I didn't even know there was milk in the fridge. How have you done this on your own for so long?"

This time, she sat in the chair across from the bed. "I wasn't always on my own, as you now know," Juniper said with a half smile. "I have friends from growing up in Wintervale. Danny and I traveled a lot before we came back to Vermont so he could go to med school in New Hampshire. We took over the farm while Danny did his residency at Hadleigh Hope, the hospital in the town right next to us. And then... you just adapt, right?"

Juniper didn't know what she said, but it made Harley's huge brown eyes tear up and she thought he was going to cry. She didn't know if she should hug him or not, but he didn't give her the option. Instead, he took a deep breath, let it out, then sipped the cocoa and smiled as he blinked the tears away.

"This is the best hot chocolate I've ever had in my life."

"It's my friend's recipe," she admitted. Juniper would have to text her friend Molly tomorrow and thank her for sharing it.

"Listen, Juniper. I'm sorry if I scared you. I didn't mean..."

She quickly interrupted him.

"No, don't apologize. Please. If you ever need anything at all, whenever, just call up to the house. I wrote the number down on that list by the landline. I don't sleep much anyway, so..." she trailed off. "I'll let you sip that and get back to sleep. Don't get up too early tomorrow, okay? Forget about the gardens. Just get to the horses whenever you can."

"Thank you, Juniper," he whispered as he looked up at her over the mug. Their eye contact lasted just a minute too long, which caused her to gently shut the door and then run from the guest house. She wrapped her robe tighter around her waist when a shiver ran down her spine. The night had suddenly grown muggy and warm, but the shiver...

It had nothing to do with the weather.

Chapter Twelve

HARLEY

I t was the end of Harley's first week at Wintervale Farms and he'd already fallen into a rhythm that felt more natural than anything had in a long time. Every morning, he would get up and take a quick shower, then go to the farmhouse to eat breakfast and watch cartoons with Enid until Frannie could come over around noon. It meant he was working during the hottest part of the day, but he was starting to get used to the different sort of heat brought on by a Vermont summer.

The one thing Harley was having a little more trouble processing was the feeling of becoming part of a family again. As he felt his walls coming down, he also was getting a little nervous. Every time Enid brought him a cup of strawberry milk, or when Juniper left a basket of peaches outside of his door, Harley felt a little bit more in love with the Farm, and the family...

But also just a little bit more scared of losing everything.

By Saturday night, all of the closeness was starting to make Harley feel a little stir crazy, so when he saw Juniper jogging over to the restaurant, he ran as fast as he could to intercept her. She jumped in surprise when he skidded across the grass and stopped directly in front of her, causing her to bump head first into his chest.

"I'm sorry," he said quickly as he helped Juniper steady herself. "I didn't mean to cut you off like that."

She took a few steps back and brushed her hair from her face.

"It's fine! Is something wrong?" she asked nervously.

"No! Everything is great. I was just wondering if I could have the day off tomorrow? I haven't had a chance to explore the town and I thought I could use the day to wander around, maybe say hi to some strangers."

Juniper hid behind her hands. "Oh, gosh. Of course! I'm sorry I didn't offer you any time off before. You've been working so hard and helping *so* much, even with things that aren't part of your job. I'll take care of the horses tomorrow. Heads up though. Since it's Sunday, a lot of the shops and stuff will be closed."

"That's fine. I just want to take a walk around and see downtown. I didn't even get the chance to drive through it when I came here. I only passed that massive resort up the mountain."

Juniper rolled her eyes. "The Mountain Wolf. If you want to make friends, don't mention it to anyone when you go to town," she said with a laugh. "But seriously. Go! Have a great time. And be warned... strangers *will* talk to you. You may not have left the farm but everyone already knows who you are."

Harley chuckled at the thought of a town full of people shaking his hand like he was the mayor.

"I'll keep it in mind," he said as she waved goodbye and went back to running towards the restaurant. Harley wasn't sure what he was looking for in downtown Wintervale, but maybe once he was there...

He would find it.

After giving himself the luxury of *really* sleeping in for the first time since he got to Vermont, Harley jumped in his truck and followed the directions Steve had given him to a restaurant called The Middle Road Inn. Even though Juniper said shops would be closed, The Middle Road Inn was packed with people grabbing Sunday brunch. All of the tables were gone when he walked in and an exasperated hostess offered a forced smile.

"Welcome to The Inn! The wait for a table is about twenty minutes, but if you don't mind eating at the bar..." she trailed off hopefully.

"The bar is just fine, thanks. I can just grab my own stool."

She sighed gratefully, handed Harley a menu, then ran back into the kitchen like there was a fire. As he wandered slowly up to the bar, he noticed the restaurant had gotten a little bit quieter, and every eye seemed to be watching him. Juniper wasn't kidding; Harley felt like the new kid at school.

He'd barely had a chance to look at the menu when a bartender appeared out of nowhere.

"What can I get for you this morning? Our brunch special today is fresh blueberry pancakes with maple syrup, your choice of eggs, and sausage or bacon. The syrup comes straight from Winter-vale Farm," he said. Harley couldn't help but laugh. Of *course* the syrup came from Juniper's farm. Was there anything she didn't do?

"The special sounds great. I'll take my eggs fried and my bacon extra crispy, please."

The bartender nodded and sped off again, leaving Harley alone at the bar to take in the scenery. The Middle Road Inn was something else; it reminded him of a pub from a fantasy film, but the walls were covered in photos of Wintervale over the last hundred years. He was lost in the history of the restaurant when, out of nowhere, a woman plopped down on the stool next to him. She had a dog by her side that was wearing a little vest and smiling up at him.

"Can I help... either of you?" Harley asked as the bartender returned with a mug of coffee for him. The woman gestured at the cup and the bartender nodded.

"You got it, Theo."

Harley turned back to her. "Theo, is it? And who is your friend?"

She gave the dog a few scratches.

"This is Portia. She's my sidekick. And you're Harley Thatcher, right?"

He couldn't help but laugh again. "I am. I know we haven't met, so I'm guessing this is what Juniper warned me about."

"It's a small town, sweetie. Everyone has been anxiously waiting for you to make your way down here. Are you settling in on the farm?"

Harley took a long sip of his black coffee. It was rich and delicious and he could feel himself waking up as the caffeine tingled at the base of his neck.

"It's beautiful. And Juniper and Enid are wonderful. Never imagined that I'd be much of a Vermont kind of guy, but it turns out, I like it up here." Harley looked down at Portia with a smile. "And what is that lovely lady's story?"

Theo lifted up the cuff of her jeans and Harley cringed when he saw it was a prosthesis. "Portia is my service dog for PTS."

I'm such a jerk.

"Hey, I'm sorry if I was nosy. It's none of my business."

She waved a hand at him dismissively as she reached across the bar and grabbed cream and sugar for her coffee. "If privacy is your thing, you came to the wrong town. Anyway, you weren't being nosy. I was an Army Ranger once upon a time. Now I'm working on getting my medical degree. But every now and then, I still have issues with post traumatic stress from the accident. So, if you ever need to talk or anything..." she trailed off.

It took Harley a second longer to catch on than he would have liked, but it was still early. When he realized it was an ambush, he laughed loudly enough to draw everyone's attention again.

"Did Juniper call you?"

Theo shrugged with a sly grin. "I promise, she was nothing but respectful. She just thought maybe you could use someone else to talk to, someone who had maybe been in your shoes before... so to speak?"

The bartender returned with Harley's food and before he could walk away, Theo reached out and grabbed the pen from his shirt pocket. He started to argue but she hushed him up quickly.

"Cool it, Andy, you'll get it back. Can you hand me a napkin?"

The bartender begrudgingly did as she asked and wandered off again. Theo jotted her name and number down on the napkin, then handed it to Harley.

"Day or night, if you need anything. You call me, okay?" Theo said, her smile warm and genuine. Harley tucked the napkin into his shirt pocket and nodded.

"Okay."

She patted his arm gently and then walked back over to a table where a man who looked like a lumberjack had been waiting patiently for her. As soon as Theo sat down, his face lit up, and he reached out to squeeze her hand. His cheeks turned pink like it was their first date, but he'd noticed the delicate engagement ring on Theo's finger. They both looked so happy. Harley couldn't remember the last time he'd allowed himself to feel happiness like that. It always felt like he was betraying the friends he lost...

Maybe he *would* call Theo later, just to see what she had to say.

Chapter Thirteen

Juniper was covering dinner again because Sebastian's grandmother had taken a turn and he needed to rush back to Burlington. He was a part of the family, so she was happy to cover, but that meant she had to take Enid over to her Aunt and Uncle's house and leave Wren & Candle in the hands of her wait staff. Even though she probably broke a land speed record getting back to the restaurant, everything was in shambles by the time Juniper got back. Tables hadn't been turned, there was a line of waiting customers out the door, and dirty dishes were being stacked outside the kitchen but not actually taken to the dishwasher.

It was going to be a long night.

Juniper was about half way through seating the customers when she looked up from the reservation book and saw Harley was standing in front of her. He was in his jeans but had on a really nice button down. His hair was still curly and damp from the shower but he was freshly shaven for the first time since Juniper had met him. He was also wearing a cologne that smelled so amazing, it made her dizzy for a second.

"Did you have a reservation?" she asked with a shy laugh.

"I was hoping I could sneak in. Once I realized there was food in the fridge, I went a little crazy snack crazy and now there is nothing left in the house. I promise, I'm not a stray cat. If you feed me tonight, I won't come sniffing around again tomorrow," he said with an uncharacteristic wink that made Juniper a little weak in the knees. She could hear customers getting impatient behind him, so she waved Harley over next to her at the host's stand, then quickly seated a four-top that had just opened up. When she got back to the front, Harley was rocking back and forth on his heels, nodding uncomfortably as he smiled at the people in line.

"Just another five minutes," Juniper said to the couple who was next up. Then she turned back to Harley as she tried to keep her "customer service" smile on. "It's my fault. I was supposed to do the shopping this morning but the day got away from me. I'm going in the morning and will grab you some groceries then. You can eat at the family table in the back tonight. Ask for tuna special, it's amazing."

As soon as she said it, they both watched as the sous chef ran up front and erased the tuna special from the black board.

"Right. Well, the ribeye..." Juniper started, but didn't get to finish her sentence because the sous chef wiped the ribeye from the blackboard next. Juniper and Harley stood there frozen for a moment to make sure nothing else was being eighty-sixed; once he finally walked away, they let out identical sighs from holding their breath.

"Okay then! Just order whatever you want off the menu and let the kitchen know. If you want to wait back there?" she asked. She wasn't trying to hurry him off, but their biggest table of the night had just arrived, and whenever he was around, she tended to act a little flighty. Juniper needed to be clear-headed for this one. But Harley didn't question her; instead, he nodded and slipped through the crowd to the back of the restaurant. That gave her a second to take a deep breath and approach Gabriel D'Arbo, who was at the front of the group.

"Mr. D'Arbo, so nice to see you again," she said to her friend Molly's father. He was the manager of The Mountain Wolf lodge in Hadleigh and thanks to his connections, the owners were considering opening another Wren & Candle at the resort. The whole executive board was there for dinner and this was a make or break thing for the possibility of branching out.

"Please, Juniper, call me Gabriel. I told my friends that they're in for a delicious dinner, *oui mon cher*?" he asked as one of the waitresses sat the executives and their partners at the family style table in the middle of the restaurant.

"It will be an amazing experience, I promise," Juniper said as Gabriel kissed her cheek and then took his own seat. Out of the corner of her eye, she saw Harley waving at her from the kitchen entrance. "Gabriel, I will leave you in the hands of my wonderful staff so you can order. And please, everyone, a round of drinks on the house. Our rosemary martini is delicious." Juniper glanced over at the bartender with daggers to make sure she didn't erase anything from the specials board. She held her hands up defensively.

Once everything was settled with the executives, she walked as calmly as she could manage back to the kitchen. Harley held up a to-go container with a smile.

"Thank you for this. I got the meatloaf. But I think I'll eat it back at the house. You're really busy here and I don't want to distract you."

You do that no matter where you are on the farm, she thought.

"What?" Harley asked. Juniper's heart dropped. Had she said that out loud?

"What?" Juniper parroted as a stalling tactic that even she wasn't buying.

"I thought you said something. Nevermind. I'll let you get back to work. And if you need help with the grocery shopping in the morning, let me know. I can get the stables done early," Harley said as he walked backwards out of the rear entrance. Juniper waved at him and responded,

"Yuh-huh!"

Once he was out of sight, she dropped her head into her hands. *What is the matter with me? Why do I keep acting like this when he is around?* She recognized that it was getting a little silly, because as soon as he was out of her sight, she actually felt like she missed him. And Juniper hadn't felt anything like that for a long time, for anyone other than Danny.

"Juniper!"

She screamed and spun around, her heart racing a mile a minute. It was one of her waitresses.

"Jeez, Tina. Are you wearing ballet slippers? Make some noise when you walk," Juniper said as she pushed her hair away from her face. "What's up?"

"The people at that table want you to tell them the ingredients of the rosemary martini," Tina said with as much enthusiasm as she could muster. Juniper scoffed.

"Not without a contract. I've got it covered, girl. Go take your break."

Tina scurried off outside and Juniper took a deep breath. Time to be the most confident person in the room again...

Whether she was feeling it or not.

Chapter Fourteen

HARLEY

I t was still early when Harley heard Juniper's truck rumble to a stop in front of his house. He had just woken up, so he threw on a shirt without buttoning it and slipped into his jeans, then walked out barefoot. When he got outside, Juniper was already unloading canvas bags from the back of her truck. She turned around, her arms loaded, and when she saw him, she jumped... dropping a few of the bags in the process.

"Aw, sh... Shiny fairy wings. I hope the milk wasn't in there," Juniper said as Harley rushed over to help her.

"Shiny fairy wings?" he asked, laughing as he took almost all of the bags from her.

"Once Enid learned how to talk, I had to stop swearing. It's a hard habit to break... Oh, crap!" she said, slapping her forehead. Harley raised his eyebrow. "Crap doesn't count. I was supposed to pick up the blankets for the fireworks before I went grocery shopping. I didn't even call Claudia..."

Harley shook his head in confusion as they walked into his house to set the groceries down. "I have no idea what you're talking about, Juniper."

"Right, sorry. You've only been in town a few times so you

may not have seen the flyers. For the 4th of July, Wintervale and Hadleigh both have fireworks displays in their parks. The first year we were open, a lot of people booked dinner here on the fourth because you could see both sets of the fireworks since we're on the border of both towns. This year, we decided to offer a package deal. So, we're offering a locally sourced buffet, a blanket for watching a show on the yard, and a concert, all for a flat price."

Even though she looked exhausted, Harley could see her eyes light up as she talked about it. And because she was excited, he was suddenly excited at the prospect of helping her.

"Hey, if you need some assistance getting things together, I can give you a little backup when my work is done. Missing a little sleep won't hurt me none. I can go get the blankets, then weed the garden when I get back?"

Juniper scrunched her forehead up suspiciously. "Why would you want to help with this? It's going to be a major headache and it's definitely not part of your job description."

Harley shrugged and smiled.

"Many hands make light work, right?"

"You're such a Texas boy," Juniper said with a chuckle. "Yeah, okay. I haven't had time to do anything I need to, so I can call the rental company about the buffet equipment. The blankets are at Claudia Monroe's dance studio on Fir Street. Her husband, Reid, owns the ice rink and they've accumulated a bit of a surplus of blankets over the years, so he's loaning them out. Anyway, follow Pine Street to the end and you'll have to turn left onto Fir. You won't be able to miss her studio. It's... pink."

Harley burst into laughter. "So, I won't look out of place?"

He could hear Juniper snort laugh as she walked toward his front door.

"You'll fit right in, I promise."

* * *

Harley parked his truck at the end of Pine Street and decided to walk back up to the coffee shop to grab an espresso. He actually *was* a little tired today and needed a boost of caffeine before he went into a dance studio full of little kids with way more energy than him. Harley walked past a bakery, a shop for handmade dresses, a cat toy store, and a few other interesting places he planned to check out on a day when he wasn't on a mission. He kept meaning to stop at Kit and Steve's antique shop too, but the days seemed to get away from him on the farm.

He was just about to round the corner to Bean There, Done That when he heard his voice being shouted from the other side of the street. He turned and saw Theo waving at him, her dog Portia by her side. They checked for traffic and then hustled over to where he was standing.

"Funny running into you down here!" she said cheerily.

"Is it though? This seems like the kind of place where you inevitably run into everyone you know all of the time."

Theo laughed when she was forced to admit he was right.

"I thought I lived in a small town in Maine but Wintervale... if nosy was a contest, Wintervale would leave every other small town in the dust. It's not the worst to suddenly have a family that's a couple of hundred people deep, and each of them would give you the shirt off their back."

Harley looked around at the people roaming the streets, smiling and shaking hands. Even the grumpiest old man inching down the street with his walker had a cheery and lovely elderly woman walking next to him, making him laugh every once in a while. Austin was a great city and it would always have his heart, but Wintervale *was* starting to feel a little bit like home.

"You never called me," Theo said suddenly, startling Harley from his thoughts.

"Right. Sorry. I guess the days just kind of got away from me."

She gestured toward Bean There. "Brady is over at his veterinary clinic. I've got some time before he's done with his emergency visit. Coffee?"

He didn't want to dawdle, because he still had to get the blankets and get back to his work at the farm. But a few minutes chatting couldn't hurt...

"Coffee sounds good, Theo. It sounds great, actually."

Chapter Fifteen

JUNIPER

Juniper had just gotten off the phone with the catering rental company when she flopped down on the couch in the living room and took a deep breath. Harley was in town, Enid was with her Aunt and Uncle, and Sebastian was covering Wren & Candle. There was an almost oppressive silence in the house and Juniper wasn't sure she was comfortable with it. Most days, she probably would claim to be grateful for a few moments of quiet to herself, but maybe that wasn't what she actually wanted. There was so much quiet after Danny... now that she had Enid's perpetual motion and the constant coming and going of people on the farm, she was pretty confident that being alone wasn't for her.

She was just about to go over to the restaurant for something to do when there was a knock on the front door. Juniper sprang to her feet and ran to the door to see who it was. When she pulled the curtain aside, she saw Frannie waving at her with one hand and a box of donuts from The Flour Girl in the other.

"Lifesaver!" Juniper said when she flung the door open. Before she gave Frannie a hug, she took the box of donuts out of her hands and took a long sniff of them, still hot from the oven. Frannie laughed at her.

"I see how important I am. Just for that, you're making the coffee."

Juniper rolled her eyes and hugged her friend. "I was going to anyway. Come on in."

Frannie dropped her giant purse on the couch and looked up the stairs.

"Where is the moppet?"

Juniper turned the coffee maker on and took two plates out of the cabinet. "With Kit and Steve. Rose is still sick and since I had a lot to get done today, they offered to have her spend the night. She gets spoiled rotten over there, so there was no argument."

"And the cowboy?" Frannie asked with a sly smile.

"Fireman," Juniper said as she shook her head and laughed. "He went to get the blankets for the 4th of July dinner from Claudia. He wants to lend a hand and I'm in no position to turn down help."

Frannie sighed as she broke apart the donut on her plate.

"You *do* know that you light up when you talk about him, right?"

Juniper froze in place with the carafe of coffee in her hand. "What are you talking about? I don't... you don't know that... he just helps with the stable!"

Frannie took the coffee pot from Juniper's hand and filled their cups while Juniper continued to stand next to the table, dumbfounded.

"Honey, I know I haven't been a part of your life as long as Claudia and Pippa and Belle. And I know I didn't have the opportunity to meet Danny. But I feel like we've gotten really close since I moved here. Juni, it's been four years. Do you really think Danny would want you to be alone forever?"

Juniper laughed, but not at Frannie's earnest question. It was at a memory of her husband the night before their wedding. They were sitting together on the porch swing out front, before the house was theirs. He hadn't decided if he was going to shave his beard in the morning yet, so Juniper snuggled up close to his scruffy face as he wrapped his arm around her. They were watching the sun set, and suddenly, Danny kissed her on the top of the head and whispered to her.

"Juni... if anything should ever happen to me, and you have the chance to move on..."

She pulled away and looked up at Danny in surprise. He never brought up things like this. "Yes?"

"Don't do it. You're never going to find anyone who loves you more than me. In fact, just wear black for the rest of your wife. And a veil. Make sure everyone knows that I'm watching and if I have to haunt them, I will."

Juniper burst out laughing and buried her head in his neck. Even four years later, she could remember the way he smelled that night, and the softness of his hair against her skin. Frannie was watching her like she was crazy now, but it had been a long time since she thought about that night, and Danny's smile still brought her so much joy.

"I'm sorry, I wasn't laughing at you. Actually, Danny made his thoughts on that point pretty clear. But for real? No, I don't think he'd be happy if he knew that I didn't even consider moving on... Until now, I guess."

Frannie clapped her hands together. "That's great! So, what are you waiting for?"

Juniper couldn't keep talking about Harley like this. It was making her stomach dance around and if it kept up, she wouldn't be able to keep her donut down.

"Enough about me. Have you and Micah set a date yet? I take it you're getting married at Wintervale Fellowship?" she asked, desperately trying to change the subject to Frannie's upcoming nuptials to the local pastor.

"Stop trying to change the subject, Juniper. Do you have feelings for Harley?"

Darn it.

"I don't really *know* Harley. All I know is that he's very kind. He makes me laugh. He's obviously handsome. I feel safe when he's close to me. But I also feel like there is something he isn't telling me, you know?"

Frannie set down her coffee mug and raised a curious eyebrow. "Did you Google him when you hired him?"

Juniper flinched.

"No..."

"Juni! What is wrong with you?"

"I did a background check on him," Juniper protested. "What else would I need to know?"

Frannie sighed and went to the living room to grab her laptop from her giant bag. She came back with it already open.

"What is his name? Where is he from?"

Juniper had to pause for a second to recall, since her mind had been so scrambled lately. "Harley... Thatcher. He came here from Austin and I think he was born around there too? He had a grandmother who passed away. That's really all he's told me."

It only took seconds for Frannie to type his info into her laptop and when the results returned, her eyes grew wide in a combination of horror and surprise.

"Oh, god. What is it? He's not a serial killer, is he?"

Frannie shook her head as tears welled in her eyes. Now Juniper was freaking out, so she snatched the laptop from Frannie's hands and spun it around in front of her. When she saw the headline from a newspaper's website in Austin, she had to read it three times to make sure she understood it.

Junkyard Explosion Rocks Downtown: Young Boy Rescued by Lone Fire Company Survivor
Emerald Li, Staff Writer

January 5, 2020

In the early morning hours of January 5, Fire Company 3, stationed near Hyde Park, answered an anonymous call regarding a fire at Carl's Junkyard. Less than an hour later, only a single member of the company would leave the junkyard alive.

While saving an underage employee of the junkyard trapped in wreckage, firefighter Harley Thatcher narrowly avoided the chemical explosion that claimed the lives of the rest of his fellow firefighters. Thatcher and the unnamed employee are currently in stable condition at St. David's Medical Center. While Thatcher was unable to be reached for comment, the parents of the employee have told local news stations that they owe Thatcher, "a debt of gratitude that can never be repaid."

The cause of the explosion is still being investigated, but sources within the arson division of Austin Police Department do not believe the fire was intentionally set. Any further information will be provided via the Fire Investigation Division of the Austin Fire Department.

This was the fourth incident at Wade's Junkyard that required emergency intervention in the last year. Neither Public Health nor OSHA were willing to comment for this story.

A memorial for the lost firefighters of Fire Company 3 is currently being planned, with a time and date to be announced soon.

By the time she finished reading, Juniper realized she'd had her hands covering her mouth the entire time.

"Oh... oh, my god. Frannie..." She knew she wasn't saying anything constructive but she couldn't seem to come up with the right words.

"I know. I actually remember seeing this come through with a batch of news stories back in January but I didn't register his name when I read it." Frannie was still a producer for a morning show that filmed in New York, so she knew just about everything that was going on in the news. Juniper was actually shocked she *didn't* remember Harley's name from the report.

"I guess that's why he wanted to get as far away from Texas as possible. I'm kind of surprised he didn't go to Alaska," she said as she ran her hands through her hair.

"He didn't, Juniper. He came here. And maybe there was a reason for that. Maybe you two were *meant* to meet each other."

She chuckled sadly. "Micah is rubbing off on you."

"Not exactly," Frannie said as she took her computer back. "But don't you think you should at least consider it?"

Juniper buried her face in her hands. Harley wasn't just the "kindly and quiet" guy who worked on her farm. He was an actual hero who had lost everyone he ever loved. She didn't exactly know how she felt about him yet, but one thing was for sure...

She was going to make sure Harley knew he had a family on Wintervale Farms, a family who would be there for him no matter what.

Chapter Sixteen

HARLEY

Harley grabbed a seat in the small coffee shop and had to wiggle around to get comfortable. He felt like he was sitting in a chair for a child; his knees were practically in his chest. When Theo sat down across from him, he felt even more conspicuous, especially when she laughed warmly at him.

"Would you rather sit at the bar? I think the stools might lower a little bit so your knees wouldn't dig into the bar."

"I feel like a fairy tale giant. Is this a coffee shop for kids?"

A brunette with huge, lovely brown eyes appeared from behind the bakery case and startled Harley.

"*Are* you a fairy tale giant?" she asked in a voice that had a slight French accent. "I think you are the tallest person I have ever met in my life."

Harley squirmed uncomfortably again. "I think I'm just a normal human, miss," he said as the brunette brought them their coffee and muffins.

"Oh, stop hassling him, Molly. You want him to come back, don't you?" Theo asked, her eyes set in a glare that caused Molly to stick her tongue out. "Ignore her. She's pregnant and cranky about being on her feet. The girl she hired to cover the shop hasn't made

73

it into town yet. So, tell me, stranger. What wakes you up screaming in the middle of the night?"

Harley laughed, though he didn't know why. Theo was so direct and he wasn't used to that. No one in Texas ever came right out and asked him how he was doing. In fact, he realized how unaccustomed he was to talking about his feelings. Mostly, he just deflected conversations about them.

"You said you had PTS but you didn't say why," Harley said, deflecting like a master. "Is it because of…" he trailed off, but gestured at her leg. Theo nodded.

"I was an Army Ranger deployed in the Middle East and we were clearing buildings of IEDs. We found a family in one of the buildings and thought we got everyone out, but a little girl got left behind. I went back for her and…" Theo made an explosion gesture with her hands. "By the time they were able to get a Medi-Vac, it was too late for my leg. I have burns down my left side and I still can't hear well out of my left ear."

Harley gulped. "And the girl?"

Theo just shook her head as tears welled in her eyes. Then she took a deep breath and let out a sad laugh.

"So, now you know my story, cowboy. Fair is fair."

For a moment, Harley felt that hard knot in his throat that showed up whenever he tried to talk about the night in the junk-yard. But Theo was watching him, waiting, and something deep inside of him said it was time to say the words out loud.

"My entire firehouse died on a call. Everyone but me."

He expected Theo to be surprised or shift directly into conso-lation mode, like everyone else who knew. Instead, she slowly nodded her head. Then, to Harley's surprise, Portia ambled over and set her head on his leg, like she anticipated that he needed a little bit of comfort.

"Did you know already?" he asked Theo.

"I didn't. I wanted to respect your privacy. But I had a feeling that it had to do with your old job. How did it happen?"

Harley told her everything about the explosion, the boy, the constant stream of condolences that weighed so heavily on him that he couldn't leave the house for a month. He even admitted that no matter where he went or what he did, he still felt like he was carrying every one of his fellow firefighters on his back, trying to drag them to safety. They were there with every step he took and *that* was his burden for surviving when they didn't.

When Theo reached out and put her hand on his, a hand that carried the scars of her own pain, he forced himself not to pull away.

"You have survivor's guilt, Harley. It's real and it is *nothing* to be ashamed of. Have you talked to a therapist since the accident?"

Harley scoffed. "That's not really my thing."

"Then make it your thing. You didn't survive because you ran away from the danger. You survived because you were saving a life. And I can guarantee you with absolute certainty that your friends would not want you to keep carrying around this burden. You can't keep living your life like you died with them."

Harley felt like he was going to cry and the impulse to run away was growing stronger by the minute. But Portia's head was still on his leg and Theo was still holding his hand and between the two of them, he felt like he was being anchored to the ground. Instead of running, he took a long, deep breath to slow the blood rushing through his head and heart. As he did, he really looked at Theo, at the sparkle in her eyes and the engagement ring on her hand. She looked exhausted, but happy, like she had fought a war and come out of the other side stronger than she started.

He wanted to feel that way too.

"A therapist, huh? That's all there is to it?"

Theo laughed as she let go of his hand to dig through her bag. "It's not a magic wand. You'll have to do a lot of hard, emotional work. But I promise that talking about it is better than keeping it bottled up inside."

After another minute of digging, Theo returned with a little card case, and from there, she pulled out a business card with a doctor's name on it.

"She specializes in post-traumatic stress and anxiety. Give her a call when you're ready."

Harley nodded as he tucked the card into his pocket, then chugged down the remainder of his coffee. "I should really get to the dance studio for those blankets. Thank you for this, Theo. It really meant a lot."

"Any time, Harley. I mean that. Did Juniper tell you how to get to Claudia's?"

Harley laughed as he offered Theo a hand to help her stand from the chair, more as a result of the gentlemanly behavior instilled in him by his grandmother than Theo's need for assistance. She took his hand graciously and nodded her thanks.

"She said just to look for a lot of pink on Fir Street?"

"That will do it," Theo said as she chuckled. "And hey, can you let Juniper know that Brady and I will be at Wren & Candle for the buffet? I think we just may skip out before the fireworks. Portia and I aren't terribly fond of them." She reached down and scratched the happy dog, who always seemed to be smiling.

"I'll let her know," Harley said as he put a few extra dollars in the tip jar for the owner, since she was the only one working. He was just about to head to the door when suddenly, Theo threw her arms around him and pulled him into a bear hug so tight, he almost couldn't breathe.

"You don't always have to be the hero, Harley. You can let people in," she whispered as she patted him gently on the back.

Harley was grateful that there wasn't anyone on the sidewalk when he got outside. He didn't want anyone to see him cry.

Chapter Seventeen

JUNIPER

There were only a few days left before the 4th of July and Juniper felt like she was crazy behind on everything. She was doing her best to handle everything herself but when it came to setting up the stage for the band, she knew there was no way she was going to get it done on her own. The pieces were still in the barn from last year, but her friends James and Brady had come over to help. It took them all day, but between the three of them, they were able to get it done. But when she called James, he was catering a lunch at the mayor's house and Brady was doing an emergency surgery on a cat. So now, it was just Juniper, standing in the barn and staring at pieces of wood and metal that she couldn't even pick up.

"Is there something I can help you with?"

Juniper spun around in surprise at the sound of Harley's voice. "No. I mean, yes. I mean... I don't want to impose."

Harley looked at her with an eyebrow raised.

"Juniper, I work for you. I can do whatever you need me to. Right now, it looks like you're trying to move those planks with telepathy and not getting very far."

She sarcastically laughed at him. "It's the stage for the band

77

and it kind of all just…" she made a confusing gesture with her hands, "smooshes together? But I can't move them alone and my usual free labor had to work at their actual jobs today."

Harley stepped in front of her and examined the biggest pieces of wood, which made up the stage. Next, he seemed to measure them with his hands before muttering a few words to himself and hoisting a plank of wood onto his shoulder like it was balsa wood.

"Where to?" he asked as Juniper stared at him in disbelief. She stumbled over her words for a moment before she seemed to regain her composure.

"That empty patch of grass in front of the vegetable gardens. I put up ropes, but inevitably some joker who had a few too many of our signature drinks will start snatching veggies."

Harley nodded and walked casually over to the garden, then set the wood down and returned for another piece. He did it over and over again, with the wood first, then the metal frame, until everything was ready to be set up. Juniper dug the tools and brackets for the frame out of the barn and jogged down to where Harley was waiting.

"This looks pretty simple, huh? Lock in the frame, anchor the boards, set up the stairs, and we're ready to rock?"

Juniper laughed as she set the tools on the ground. "Rock is probably a little strong. The band this year is a bluegrass group who will play almost any event for free, just because they like the experience. My restaurant manager, Sebastian, plays mandolin. They're actually really good."

Harley nodded as if he were listening, but he had already started to connect two pieces of the frame while Juniper was talking.

"Can you come hold this side for me? I want to make sure the planks are in there good and tight."

She walked up next to where he was standing and Harley positioned her where he needed her, which meant that they were suddenly very close. Juniper felt her heart start to race the closer

Harley got to her, and then, their noses were only a couple inches apart.

"Harley, I don't…"

He didn't say anything; instead, he rested his forehead against hers, and for a moment, Juniper thought she could read his mind.

Say it's okay… say it's okay for me to kiss you…

And then, as if she had lost control of her entire body, Juniper was backing away, her legs disobeying the very adamant objections of her heart.

"Juniper? I'm sorry. I didn't meet to do anything to upset you."

She couldn't open her mouth, because if she did, she knew she would cry. She just shook her head and tried to force a smile that would let Harley know it wasn't his fault. Juniper had a feeling that wasn't the message he received as she ran into the house and slammed the door shut behind her. Rose and Enid were playing in the living room and they both looked up in surprise.

"Juni? Are you okay? You look all flushed and sweaty," Rose asked.

"Are you sick now too, mommy?" Enid followed up, holding out one of her favorite stuffed animals to her mom like it was going to cure her. Juniper forced a smile.

"I'm fine. Mommy is fine. I just need a few minutes upstairs. Are you okay?"

They both nodded but Rose mouthed, "are *you* okay?" so Enid wouldn't hear. Juniper nodded back and took the stairs up to her room two at a time. Once she was in her room with the door shut behind her, she went into her closet and retrieved a cherry wood box that Uncle Steve made her when she was a little girl. She took the box over to her bed, turned the little gold key on the front, and when the top opened, Juniper fell head first into a rabbit hole of memories.

There was a weird keychain of a duck in an inner-tube that Danny won her at a carnival, a dried rose from the first bouquet of flowers he ever bought her, her wedding and engagement rings that she'd only just taken off the year before, Danny's ring, and pictures. There were so many pictures. She hadn't been able to bring herself to look at them in years. But now... she couldn't look away.

Juniper picked them up and examined each one slowly. There was a photo of Danny leaning against the railing of the Staten Island Ferry, with Manhattan behind him, on the weekend trip they took when they found out Juniper was pregnant. He wasn't just smiling; he was glowing. Usually when she looked at the picture, the tears would roll down her cheeks before she even realized she was crying. But now, she was smiling back at him. When Danny found out he was going to be a father, the light inside of him glowed even brighter. His smile that day was one of Juniper's favorite memories.

As she took picture after picture from the box, and touched each of them lovingly, she realized that she wasn't sad anymore. She missed Danny, she would *always* miss him, but the memories didn't break her heart anymore. Even when she got to a picture of them holding Enid's sonogram from the dinner at The Middle Road Inn the night they told their friends Juniper was pregnant, all she felt was love. Her heart was full of love, and despite his joke the night before their wedding, she knew that Danny wouldn't want her to bottle that love up for the rest of her life.

Juniper picked up Danny's wedding ring and held it tight in her hand as she crawled off the bed to peek out the window. Harley was already building the top of the stage with the wood planks. She couldn't believe how quickly he'd gotten the whole thing together. She also couldn't help but notice how handsome he looked, bathed in the orange glow of the sunset. Juniper knew deep down that it was time for her to let go of her grief and move on...

But *could* Harley be that man?

Chapter Eighteen

HARLEY

Harley had a really weird night.

The whole time he'd worked on the stage, he couldn't stop thinking about Juniper. He'd accidentally slammed the hammer down on his hand three times because he was so distracted. How could he have messed everything up so badly in so little time? He was sure in that moment that they were feeling the same thing and then she ran away like he was a wolf descending on her in the woods. Even his clumsy attempt at an apology didn't seem to make a difference. Once the stage was done, he thought about going to the farmhouse to try and apologize again. But then he saw that Rose's car never left, which meant she was sleeping over, and Harley couldn't bear to face Rose, Enid, *and* Juniper at the same time.

After he checked on the horses one last time for the night, Harley went back to the guest house and picked at some leftovers from Wren & Candle, though he didn't have much of an appetite. Once he was done, he turned on the TV to an old movie and paced around the living room. Once in a while, he would peek out through the curtains to get a look at the farmhouse. As soon as all of the lights went out, he flopped down on his bed in resignation.

He had blown it. Harley wouldn't have been surprised if Juniper sent him packing first thing in the morning.

He wasn't sure what time he passed out, but it was after 2am when he was awoken from a dead sleep by a familiar smell. It immediately sparked every nerve in his body and he sat up like a bloodhound who just caught a scent on a trail...

Smoke.

Harley jumped to his feet and turned on the nearest lamp to check the space around him for fire, but everything inside was normal. The TV was still lightly humming with a different black and white movie and the kitchen was bathed in undisturbed moonlight. That meant the smoke was coming from outside; Harley was already putting on his boots when he heard the sound of the horses snorting and squealing from the stable. He swore out loud as he ran out the front door, pulling his shirt over his head as he went.

As soon as he was outside, Harley saw the smoke billowing up around the left side of the stable.

"Harley!"

Juniper and Rose were running across the yard in their pajamas. They were only half-awake, but Harley could see the terror in Juniper's eyes.

"Stay there! Don't come any closer," he yelled to them as he ran for the right side of the stable. The tops of the doors were open, so there was smoke coming out, but it was obvious the fire was on the left by the supplies. The first thing Harley did was dip a bandana from his jeans in a bucket of water, then he tied it around his face. Once that was secure, he ran inside of the stable, opening every stall so the horses could charge out into the meadow.

When he got to the last stall, Magic seemed to be frozen by her fear. The smoke was thickest by her and now Harley could see the occasional flash of orange cutting through gray. There wasn't much time. He slid into the stall beside Magic and put his arms around her neck.

"Come on, girl," Harley whispered. "Come on. Enid is waiting for you. You can't let her down. Let's get out of here."

Magic let out a light whicker and followed Harley out of her stall. Once she realized there was an escape, she didn't need any further encouragement. Once he saw the palomino was safe in the meadow, Harley ran back and grabbed the fire extinguisher that was kept at either door. As he sprayed down the fire in front of him, he could see that whatever had started it was coming from the roof. Even though he was able to put out the flames on the ground, there wasn't enough in the extinguisher to reach the beams at the top of the stable.

His only option now was the hose on the other side.

There was virtually no water from the stable's spout, so it was mostly used for filling water troughs and baths. Now, Harley had to use it to put out a fire that could spread again at any moment.

"I called 911! Don't go back in there, Harley!" Juniper shouted to him over the deafening roar of the fire and the cries of the still-spooked horses. But he wasn't thinking like a civilian now. There was a fire in front of him and it needed to be put out. He couldn't let Juniper's stable burn down. It wasn't an option.

Harley turned the water on as high as it would go, wet his bandana again, and ran into the left side of the barn. The beams were already burning to the point that they could give out at any minute, so he covered half of the spout and created the best stream of water he could. It didn't take long for Harley's eyes to burn and water, but he was so close... he could see the flames giving way to more smoke. He could just hear the sound of sirens in the distance when the last of the fire was gone. Nothing was left but billows of smoke and the charred remains of the supply closet.

With an exhausted cough, Harley dropped the hose and tumbled out onto the grass in front of the stable. He was staring up at the sky, the stars obscured by clouds of smoke, when Juniper appeared over him. She pulled the bandana away from his face and tossed it off to the side.

"Are you okay? Are you breathing? Say something," she said as she brushed his hair away from his face. He coughed again and sat up on his elbows.

"I think I saved two-thirds of the stable," Harley answered before coughing so hard, he thought he saw ash come out of his mouth. Juniper pulled him into an unexpected hug and held him close.

"You're crazy, Harley! Why did you go back in there once the horses were out? It's just a stable! You could have died!" She was yelling at him like he was a child and he couldn't help but laugh, which only made Juniper more angry. "What exactly is so funny?"

"I was just doing my job, miss," he said as he tipped an imaginary hat.

Juniper rolled her eyes, but wasn't able to contain her smile. "If you hadn't been here..."

"I'm glad I was."

This time, it was Juniper who leaned in to kiss *him*, and neither of them even hesitated. The fire engines were pulling up and their kiss only lasted for a moment, but in that moment...

Harley knew he really *was* exactly where he belonged.

Chapter Nineteen

JUNIPER

The sun was just starting to set over Wintervale Farms as Sebastian and his band began to play. People were laying down blankets on the meadow, then loading up plates with fried chicken, lobster tacos, vegetarian pasta made with fresh veggies from the garden, and enough sides and desserts to feed an army. Juniper stood next to the back entrance of Wren & Candle, saying hello to everyone and fielding a million questions about the stable.

It hadn't taken long that night for the firefighters to figure out the fire was started by an electrical short in the lighting. If not for Harley's quick action, they could have lost not just the stable, but all of their beloved horses. Juniper had no idea how she could ever repay him, but as she watched him play with Enid and her friends on the swing set, she realized she didn't have to rush. There was a whole new life ahead of them and this time, she wouldn't take a moment of it for granted.

"What are you looking at, lady?"

Theo wandered up to Juniper with a knowing smile on her face, waking her from her daydream.

"A surprise," Juniper said as she softly laughed. "Are you heading out soon?"

Theo stuck her finger in her mouth and then held it up in the air.

"Feels like it's about that time. Can I steal some to-go containers so we can finish up at home? Brady got caught up talking to Reid about their new dog and he barely touched his food."

Juniper laughed as she reached behind the counter next to her for their specially designed biodegradable takeout containers. "So... I hear you've been talking to Harley?" she asked hesitantly. She knew that Theo wouldn't betray Harley's confidence but he'd opened up to Juniper a little bit that night after the fire and she wanted to make sure he had a support system in place.

"I have and don't you worry. That mountain of a man is way more sensitive than he seems. I think you've given him something he really needed and it's helping him work through the accident."

Juniper raised her eyebrows in surprise. "Me? What have I given him?"

"A family. And it's not just about you, or Enid, or Rose. It's all of us. He knows that we're all here for him, even if he hasn't met all of us yet. Hey, we're up in everyone's business, we take care of each other, we support each other. If that's not a family, what is?"

Juniper thought about Danny and felt her eyes well up with tears. When he died, she thought she lost the person who anchored her. But it was Kit and Steve, Belle and James, and the rest of her friends in Wintervale who lifted her up and helped her find peace again. Maybe they *were* just what Harley needed to move forward, too.

"I have to get out of here, girl. I'll call you tomorrow!" Theo said as she rushed off in Brady's direction with Portia on her heels. Juniper looked around the restaurant to make sure no one was lingering inside, then made her way out to Harley and the kids. When he saw her coming, his eyes seemed to light up.

"Time for some fireworks?" he asked as he gave Enid a push on the swing.

"Almost! Kids, why don't you go find your parents? Enid, your Aunt Kit and Uncle Steve are up by the house. Go grab a seat with them. I'll be over in a minute," Juniper said as her daughter leapt off the swing and ran off. Once they were alone, she walked up to Harley and took a long, deep breath.

"So... I know we only talked about a six month contract initially, but I was wondering if you'd stay and help me rebuild the stable? It's going to be a lot of work and I'm not sure I can do it alone."

Harley sat on the swing and gestured for Juniper to take the seat next to him. When she sat down, he reached out and took her hand in his, their fingers intertwining.

"I'll stay as long as you want and fix up whatever you need me to."

Just as he squeezed her hand, the first burst of fireworks went off from the Hadleigh side of the farm. As Juniper looked out over her home, at her daughter and her family, and then into Harley's eyes...

She knew her life was about to change forever.

Epilogue

JUNIPER - THANKSGIVING

It was the first Thanksgiving Juniper had hosted at the farmhouse since Enid was born and it was every bit as chaotic and wonderful as she hoped it would be. Steve and Kit were there, so were Rose and her parents, and Theo and Brady had stopped by with Portia. Enid was running around with Brady and playing tag which would have driven Juniper crazy any other day of the year. But on Thanksgiving, there was nothing she loved more than a packed house, full of family and friends, and the smell of amazing food cooking away in her kitchen.

It was also different this year because Harley was by her side, helping her in the kitchen. He had slowly begun to learn how to cook and took great pleasure in creating their side dishes for dinner when they ate at the farmhouse. Today, he was in charge of mashed potatoes, fresh cranberry sauce, and yams. Juniper was basting the turkey when she felt someone walk by her and thought it was Harley.

"Can you hand me that towel, hon? I need to turn the turkey around."

"Whatever you need, babe," Theo said jokingly as Juniper

jumped up in surprise, almost hitting her head on the oven. "Sorry, I didn't mean to startle you."

"I thought you were Harley."

Theo snort laughed. "I can see how you would confuse the two of us."

"Just hand me the towel, goofball."

Theo did as she asked, then waited until Juniper was back at the oven before she asked a question.

"How is progress going on the Wren & Candle at The Mountain Wolf?"

Juniper and the Mountain Wolf executives had finally reached a deal on opening a satellite restaurant right before Halloween. They were converting an empty space in the lodge itself into a bistro-sized version of Wren & Candle and they intended to make it the hottest ticket in Hadleigh. She was going to hand off management duties at the Wintervale Farms location to Sebastian and then spend six months helping them get set up in Hadleigh.

"It's going. I'm starting there in January once the interior is done. Gabriel is looking after things until I'm there every day."

Suddenly, the sound of Brady screaming out in pain echoed through the house. A collection of cleverly coded curse words preceded him yelling out, "Theo! I tripped over the rug!" She rolled her eyes and hurried out into the living room where the game of tag had gotten brutal, apparently.

Juniper was laughing to herself when Harley walked up behind her. She was sure it was him this time, because he wrapped his arms around her waist and he pulled her close.

"Juni... there is something I need to ask you, while we're alone for a second," he whispered to her. Just as she turned around, Enid came charging around the corner at top speed and slammed into Harley's back. When she hit him, a small white box flew out of his hand, careened to the floor, and slid into Juniper's foot. She bent down and picked it up, her hand shaking the whole time.

"Harley? What is this?"

He gently snatched it back from her hand and opened it, completely unaware that they had an audience now.

"This... is my grandmother's engagement ring. It's the only thing I have left of her. And I want you to have it. I love you. And I love Enid. I want to be a part of your lives, the life you started with Danny, if you will give me the honor. I want to take care of you, of Enid, of the farm, for him. Juniper Larson... will you marry me?"

She looked up at him in surprise, then down at the gorgeous antique ring, then back at him, tears already pouring down her cheeks. She didn't even have to think about it.

"Yes, Harley. Yes, I'll marry you."

All at once, everyone in the house was clapping and cheering, which made them both laugh through tears of happiness. Harley bent down and picked up Enid, then pulled Juniper back into his arms. As he held them both tight, like they were the most precious things in the world, Juniper knew that this year...

She was finally going to get her second chance at love.

WREN & CANDLE'S GROWNUP
STRAWBERRY MILK

This recipe is a delicious and versatile treat that can be adapted several different ways, making it the perfect fresh beverage for grownups or something yummy for kids (just leave out the liquor, of course)! Do you like milkshakes? Toss it in a blender with some ice

cream for a Spiked Summer Strawberry Milkshake! Are you a sucker for a strawberry dipped in chocolate? Add a shot of your favorite chocolate liqueur! No matter how you enjoy it, it will be delectable.

Ingredients:

    1 quart of fresh strawberries

    3 tsps of sugar

    1 tsp of pure vanilla extract

    1 pinch of sea salt

    4 cups of cold milk (of your choice! Any milk substitute will work)

    ¼ strawberry liqueur

    1 shot marshmallow vodka

Instructions:

1. Process strawberries and sugar in a food processor (or blender) until the mixture is smooth

2. Push mixture through a mesh strainer until only pulp is left (discard or compost pulp)

3. Add vanilla and salt to the strawberry mixture, then add the strawberries to your milk

4. Refrigerate for at least one hour (up to three days)

5. Add liqueur immediately before serving and serve with a sprig of fresh mint!

The Wintervale Promises Series

Discover more about the entire *Wintervale Promises* series at:
www.melodiemarch.com

Author photo by Crissha Figarella

Melodie March is a dreamer and a lover of nature who grew up in Vermont and can't imagine living anywhere else. When she isn't writing, she is drinking tea on her porch or volunteering at her local animal shelter. She could never pick a favorite holiday, but every winter, she's the first to start decorating her old farmhouse. She lives in Vermont on her very own Pine Street with her husband and rescue yellow labs, Honey and Lemon. If you'd like to contact Melodie to ask about your favorite Wintervale Promises character, tell her your best Christmas story, or just have a question, join her on Facebook!